MW01257360

EMMA ON FIRE

EMMA ON FIRE

JAMES PATTERSON

AND EMILY RAYMOND

Little, Brown and Company
New York Boston London

Copyright © 2025 by James Patterson

Hachette Book Group supports the right to free expression and the value of copyright. The purpose of copyright is to encourage writers and artists to produce the creative works that enrich our culture.

The scanning, uploading, and distribution of this book without permission is a theft of the author's intellectual property. If you would like permission to use material from the book (other than for review purposes), please contact permissions@hbgusa.com. Thank you for your support of the author's rights.

Little, Brown and Company
Hachette Book Group
1290 Avenue of the Americas, New York, NY 10104
littlebrown.com

First Edition: August 2025

Little, Brown and Company is a division of Hachette Book Group, Inc. The Little, Brown name and logo are trademarks of Hachette Book Group, Inc.

The publisher is not responsible for websites (or their content) that are not owned by the publisher.

The Hachette Speakers Bureau provides a wide range of authors for speaking events. To find out more, go to hachettespeakersbureau.com or email hachettespeakers@hbgusa.com.

Little, Brown and Company books may be purchased in bulk for business, educational, or promotional use. For information, please contact your local bookseller or the Hachette Book Group Special Markets Department at special.markets@hbgusa.com.

ISBN 9781538758700 (paperback) / 9780316589123 (large print)
Library of Congress Control Number: 2024952256

10 9 8 7 6 5 4 3 2 1

CCR

Printed in the United States of America

The characters and events in this book are fictitious. Any similarity to real persons, living or dead, is coincidental and not intended by the author. Please be aware that this book contains multiple references to suicide, suicidal ideation, self-harm, and depression.

EMMA ON FIRE

CHAPTER 1

Four days before the fire

EMMA CAROLINE BLAKE decides to drop the bomb in third-period AP English.

It's not a literal bomb, obviously. It won't blow up any buildings; it's not even going to knock over a desk. But it will, she hopes, destroy *something*, which is the smug complacency of literally everyone here at Ridgemont Academy, an extremely elite, extremely expensive prep school in the foothills of New Hampshire's White Mountains.

On this beautiful spring day, six weeks before graduation, Emma is completing the first homework she's done this semester—unless you count reading, which Emma doesn't. Reading isn't work; reading is escape. It's an essay that Emma spent an entire week researching, then all night writing in a Monster Energy–powered blur.

It's also the first time in a long time that Emma has felt like something that was happening at Ridgemont Academy *actually mattered.* She couldn't participate in the excitement of the lacrosse team (once again) being on a winning streak, or the daughters of the one-percenters giggling behind their phones while they snapped pics of the "blue-collar hot" boy who had been hired to muck out stalls.

Mr. Montgomery, their young, bookishly handsome teacher, gave them the assignment as a break. (A break at Ridgemont doesn't mean *no* homework; it means slightly *easier* homework.) He told them that because everyone had written such excellent critical essays on *Anna Karenina*, they deserved to have some fun with a descriptive essay.

Fun didn't really seem like the right word, if you asked Emma, but since she hadn't written an *Anna Karenina* essay at all, she felt like it was best to keep her mouth shut.

"Describe your socks," Mr. Montgomery said, "or your first car, or the way the sun sets over the ocean, or what it feels like to be caught in a rainstorm. Use your personal experience! Be creative! Don't forget specific, concrete details and descriptive language!" He seemed so excited, talking about it. Like he couldn't wait to see what they'd come up with.

Emma considered fulfilling the essay requirements by using descriptive language and concrete details about the videos that her roommate, Olivia, uploaded to her OnlyFans account, but she ultimately decided that yet another naked teenage girl on the Internet wasn't really the shake-up that Ridgemont needed.

Now, sitting in his class, feeling the warm breeze like sandpaper on her skin, Emma feels certain Mr. Montgomery is not going to like what she came up with. Which is totally fine with her. In fact, it's kind of the point.

At the front of the room, nerdy, yellow-haired Rhaina Johnson is reading about her antique French horn and how she feels when trying to play Richard Strauss's Alpine Symphony on it. The rest of the class is totally distracted, although a few students giggle when Rhaina describes the experience as "ecstatic."

"It's probably the closest she'll ever get to an orgasm, amiright?"

Emma overhears Nathaniel "Chewy" Ballantine whispering this to same-named Nathaniel "Nate" Gourdet. Nate snorts appreciatively, not noticing Emma glaring at them. Not that he'd care if he did. Once upon a time, a scathing glance from Emma Blake would have meant something. But all kinds of things have changed.

Not one of them, Emma would note, for the better.

When Rhaina finishes her essay, Mr. Montgomery leads the class in a round of applause, increasing his in volume and enthusiasm to get his students to follow suit.

"All right," he says, "who's up next?" He looks hopefully around the room.

Usually half a dozen hands would shoot up. But no one's thinking about school for once; everyone just wants to be outside in the golden April sunshine.

Finally, Emma lifts her hand. Mr. Montgomery looks surprised.

"Emma?" he asks. "Are we participating today?" He sounds so hopeful, so relieved. It's been months since she's volunteered for anything.

She imagines his own descriptive essay, the one he'll submit with his doctorate application, about how he really made a difference in this one girl's life. This girl who had obviously been hurting for so long. This girl who just needed the spiritual cleansing of a descriptive essay to restore all of her emotional balance and return her to her former glory.

"We are," Emma says.

Mr. Montgomery smiles. "I'm so glad to hear it."

Pretty soon he won't be. Pretty soon he'll be worried about whether he's even going to be allowed to continue teaching at Ridgemont, let alone getting his doctorate in being intuitively connected to his students.

Emma picks up her essay and walks to the front of the room. When she turns to face the class, they look a little more interested than they did when Rhaina was reading.

And they should. Because what she's got is better than French horns and outdated composers. What she's got will get a full-page spread in the yearbook, along with the heading "Local Tragedy Highlights Global Problems."

Chewy blows her a kiss from the back row, and Emma rolls her eyes at him. He can't help himself, he'll flirt with a brick wall.

She stands up straighter. Clears her throat. "Trigger warning, guys," she says. "My topic today"—she offers them a quick, false smile—"is self-immolation."

CHAPTER 2

SHE HEARS MR. MONTGOMERY give a quick, sharp inhale. Chewy goes, "Self-immo*what*?"

Emma makes a mostly successful effort to not roll her eyes again. Poor Chewy. He's hot, with kind of a young Chris Pine vibe, but he's also basically an idiot. He would've never gotten into Ridgemont if he weren't legacy. If his parents hadn't promised a new wing for the athletics building.

What makes Emma feel a little bit sorry for him is that he *knows* this. She can see it in the slightly apologetic way he turns in his assignments, and how he talks loudly about anything and everything he can think of (usually boobs) whenever he passes the construction site, with its sign that reads COMING SOON: BALLANTINE ATHLETICS FIELD HOUSE.

"Don't worry, Chewy," she says. "You'll understand in a

sec. This is a descriptive essay, after all. It's got a lot of visuals, which I understand boys are geared for."

Chewy smiles and nods. "Visuals. Sweet."

Emma looks down at her essay. It's three pages long, typed in Garamond (her favorite font), and practically overflowing with specific, concrete details, just like Mr. Montgomery wanted.

She clears her throat again. Her hands shake a little. But she finds the courage to begin. The question is, will she be allowed to finish?

She's written her essay exactly the way it should be, open to close: an attention-grabbing statement, followed by a walk-through of the elements she is proposing, and then an explanation of *why*. Emma is very aware that the shock value of her first line might have the power to knock Mr. Montgomery off his heels. She just needs him to stay that way until she gets to the all-important explanation.

"Four days from now, I will lock myself inside a Ridgemont Academy room, where I will set myself on fire," Emma says evenly. "My essay today will describe exactly what will happen to me, and ultimately explain why I would choose to engage in a very public social suicide."

Chewy's mouth drops open.

Mr. Montgomery barks, "Emma, what, wait—"

But she ignores him completely. She imagines that she's alone, reading out loud to herself, just like she did last night at 3:00 a.m. She practiced her performance a dozen times, ignoring the light snores that crept out from under Olivia's CPAP mask—something that hasn't made it into her Only-Fans stream yet.

No one can accuse Emma of not taking the assignment seriously. She just needs to make sure everyone understands exactly how serious she is.

"Fire needs fuel to burn," Emma reads, "so my first step will be to douse myself in gasoline. While there are numerous other flammable liquids I could use, including paint thinner, lighter fluid, and nail polish remover, gasoline has a low flash point and burns extremely hot, so that's what I'm going with. Also, it's just kind of *classic.*"

She is dimly aware of the room getting noisier, of the sound of Mr. Montgomery pushing back his rolling desk chair. She keeps on reading. "Fire needs oxygen, too, so I'll be wearing loose-fitting cotton clothing. Linen would work, but linen takes too much time to iron, and I want to look my best at my burning, although I'm not sure what filter works best with flames." She smiles ever so slightly at her joke, but she doesn't look up. She's pretty sure no one will be smiling back. Instead, she imagines they are all gaping at one another, all of them asking with their eyes, *Is she serious?*

And, oh yes. She is.

"When I light my vintage Zippo (thanks, Grandpa) and

hold the flame against my sleeve, my shirt will catch instantly. The fire will quickly spread across my chest and shoulders and down my legs. In a matter of seconds, blisters will erupt on my skin. My hair will ignite."

In a crown of flames, she wanted to write, but then she crossed it out because it sounded too pretentious, which is exactly what she doesn't want—to be one of them, lost in their own success story, not aware that the microcosm of their elite lives is built on a crumbling foundation.

She risks a glance at Chewy. The shock on his face makes him look even dumber than usual—whether that's because he still hasn't figured out what self-immolation is or he's having to grapple with his first experience of being concerned for another human being, Emma's not sure. Either way, he's still hot.

"The pain will be the worst at the beginning," Emma says, "before my nerves die. But I know that I won't have to bear the pain too long. The smoke and fumes entering my respiratory tract will kill me quickly, if shock doesn't do it first. Either way, I'll die in a matter of minutes. Excruciating, agonizing minutes, sure—but minutes nonetheless."

Spencer Jenkins goes, "That's so *sick*!"

Out of the corner of her eye, she can see Mr. Montgomery hurrying toward her from the back of the room. "Emma," he's saying, "Emma, that's enough!"

She raises her voice. Starts to read faster. "I won't stop

burning when I'd dead, though. The heat of the fire will make my skin shrink and split open. This will expose my subcutaneous fat, which is an excellent fuel source. The fat renders out—it liquefies, just like butter in a hot pan!—and then it's absorbed into whatever surface I'm on."

But now Mr. Montgomery is right in front of her, and he's got his hands on her upper arms and he's pushing her toward the door. Emma doesn't try to resist, but she doesn't stop talking either. Good thing she has the essay memorized. "This is known as the wick effect," she calls over his shoulder. "Now, *muscle* is much harder to burn than fat, and bone is even harder than—"

But now he's maneuvered her into the hallway and kicked the door shut behind them. He stares at her, his face white with shock. She can smell the cologne on his neck and the coffee on his breath. She has the wild, fleeting thought that Lizzie Grunwald would die of jealousy if she saw them right now, because Lizzie's had a crush on Mr. Montgomery ever since the very first day of school.

Even with the door shut, Emma can hear the uproar she's caused in the classroom. People asking if others think she means it, boys debating if her clothes will burn off before her skin blisters and if that'll be sexy or not, and someone telling Rhaina that her thoughts about French horns still matter.

It's exactly what Emma wanted. But the problem is that

she's not *done*. She has another page and a half of her essay to go—the part where she explains *why*.

"What the hell do you think you're doing?" Mr. Montgomery hisses.

"I'm reading my essay, like you told me to," she says calmly. "Aren't you going to let me finish?"

"No, I am not!" Mr. Montgomery bristles. "How could you read something like that?"

"You said we could pick any topic we wanted," she points out. "We just needed to include lots of specifics and details."

"I said you should write about the beach!" he cries. "Or your pets!"

"You didn't tell us things we couldn't write about it. And to be fair, I *did* give a warning."

"How can you not understand how inappropriate this is?" His hands are tightening on her shoulders, his grip starting to hurt.

And while Emma can't deny Lizzie Grunwald's assertion that Mr. Montgomery is "bookishly handsome," she also can't get past the fact that she just announced her intention to set herself on fire, and he's worried about the inappropriateness of the situation. Not, you know, her actual physical safety.

"Maybe if you had let me finish, you'd feel differently." Emma tries to move toward the door again. She wants to get to the essay's conclusion—that's the entire point. She needs everyone to hear it. "If you understand my motivation—"

Mr. Montgomery grabs the essay from Emma. "You are not going to finish." He practically spits his words in her face. "We are going to see the headmaster. Now."

CHAPTER 3

MR. MONTGOMERY'S LONG fingers keep their hold on Emma's biceps as he guides her down the hall, out the door, and across the quad to the administration building.

With its gray stone facade softened by climbing ivy and purple wisteria, Pemberly Hall looks like an English manor house. Like the setting of a romance novel or a cozy mystery—the kind of books Emma's mother used to devour when she thought no one was looking.

But there's nothing romantic or mysterious about being marched to the headmaster's office by a furious AP English teacher. They stop in front of the desk of the headmaster's assistant, Fiona Dundy. On the wall behind her hangs a poster that reads EDISCERE. SCIRE. AGERE. **VINCERE.** It's Ridgemont's motto, and it means "Study. Know. Act. **Win**."

Of course winning would be the ultimate goal of any Ridgemont graduate, and if Emma had been allowed to finish her essay, Mr. Montgomery would understand why her goal of self-immolation would ultimately be a win—maybe not for her, but for the world.

Ms. Dundy smiles brightly and says, "Oh, hello, sorry, Mr. Hastings is in a meeting."

Her eyes slide to Emma, the sheen of her irises shifting into a slightly glazed look, the one that all the staff greet Emma with now. It is a careful look, one designed to measure the impact—or possibly repercussions—of speaking to Emma Blake.

But then her gaze shifts to Mr. Montgomery's hand, still holding Emma's upper arm tightly. Ms. Dundy's mouth tightens, and Mr. Montgomery releases her.

"I don't mean to be so brusque," Mr. Montgomery says. "But I am very concerned about Emma."

"Correction," Emma speaks up. "He's concerned about inappropriateness, not me. Not really."

"You *are* inappropriate," Montgomery snaps, spinning back to her.

"What you're seeing now is not an example of how our staff typically speaks to students," a deep voice says, and the English teacher goes pale.

Emma turns to see the headmaster.

Peregrine "Perry" Hastings is standing in the doorway

of his office, flanked by a man and woman who—judging by their expensive clothes and hopeful expressions—have come to explore the possibility of their precious child attending Ridgemont Academy.

"I wouldn't be overly concerned about how staff speak to students here," Emma informs them. "Less than ten percent of applicants get into Ridgemont. But I'm sure you can find another overpriced school where free thought and expression are stifled."

"Emma!" Mr. Hastings says sharply, then turns to the parents. "I'm so sorry. I apologize for the behavior of both Ms. Blake and Mr. Montgomery. Unfortunately, Emma has been going through some challenging life changes—"

Emma snorts. "Talk about a descriptive essay."

As Mr. Hastings politely ushers Mom and Dad back into the reception area, Emma does have to give him some credit. He didn't provide any sort of excuse for her English teacher's behavior—only hers. A seed of hope blooms inside her chest. Maybe there's a chance the headmaster will hear her out.

But Mr. Hastings's politeness vanishes the instant the door shuts behind the visiting parents. "You two. Inside. Now." He snaps his fingers in a way that must have been taught at an Ivy League school back in his day...but only to the male students, of course.

Inside his office, Emma drops into a vacated club

chair. Mr. Montgomery remains standing, shifting from foot to foot in agitation and running his hand through his thick blondish hair. Mr. Hastings sits behind his mahogany desk, his stern gaze focused on Emma's English teacher.

"What could possibly have you so agitated as to behave that way in front of prospective parents?"

"Basically, I did my homework really, really well," Emma pipes up.

"Ms. Blake read an extremely inappropriate and upsetting essay to my class just now," Mr. Montgomery says, shooting her a hard look. "I don't know who to be worried about more—her or the rest of the students, who are in a state of shock."

"Better than being in a state of slumber," Emma mutters. "Which is where they were before I started reading."

Mr. Hastings pushes his pale, bushy eyebrows together. There is far more hair on his forehead than above it. "What was the subject matter?"

"Why don't you tell him, Emma?" Mr. Montgomery says.

"Why don't you?" she counters.

Emma sees a vein pulsating at Mr. Montgomery's temple. He's sort of cute when he's pissed. She can almost see why Lizzie's so in love with him—either that or she herself only finds angry people attractive, which is totally possible given her concern for the *lack* of concern she sees everywhere else.

"Ms. Blake!" Mr. Hastings barks.

Emma blinks and returns her attention to the room. She crosses her long legs and tucks her hair behind her ears. She's still mad that she didn't get to finish reading her essay, but maybe she shouldn't be so surprised. Sometimes someone puts a pin back into a grenade; sometimes a bomb gets caught right before it hits the ground.

She decides to be the picture of calm. "Mr. Montgomery assigned us a descriptive essay," she says evenly. "He said that we should use lots of details and description. So I did."

"What did you describe?"

"I described what happens to a person when they set themselves on fire."

Mr. Hastings visibly flinches, the eyebrows that had been drawn together now going up in surprise. She's not enjoying the men's discomfort, but she's not *not* enjoying it either.

"That isn't even accurate!" Mr. Montgomery cries. "She said she was going to set herself on fire. Here, at *Ridgemont Academy*."

The way he adds this particular detail—putting the emphasis on *Ridgemont Academy* instead of on *her*—makes Emma wonder if he'd be quite as upset if she'd declared her intention to do it off campus.

"Fine," Emma concedes. "I did say that I was going to

burn myself alive. The essay was well written, though, if I do say so myself."

Unlike Mr. Montgomery, Mr. Hastings keeps his outward composure. "Emma, this is very distressing," he says. "I'm shocked to hear this."

"Are you, though?" Emma asks lightly. "I'm sure you've heard the rumors. 'Emma Blake's not herself lately.' 'Emma Blake's been going downhill all semester.' I'm not exactly bearing out our motto, am I? No big win at the end for this girl." She points at herself with double thumbs, now definitely enjoying their discomfort.

Mr. Hastings and Mr. Montgomery make eye contact over Emma's head. Emma imagines them communicating via some academic ESP.

Montgomery: She's failing my class.

Hastings: She's failing philosophy too. She quit the tennis team and the teen mentor program.

Montgomery: I never see her with any of her friends. It seems like she's falling apart.

Hastings: Then we will tape her back together. We are Ridgemont Strong!

Mr. Hastings finally tears his gaze away from Mr. Montgomery and folds his hands together over his giant desk, and Emma braces herself for a barrage of meaningless words and empty promises.

"Let's set aside, for a moment, the question of

self-immolation," Mr. Hastings says. "Let's take a step back to reason and rationality. When someone like you—a straight-A student and a community leader—suddenly begins to disengage with school, we find ourselves asking why."

Emma has been expecting anger, shock, some sort of sermon about how setting yourself on fire isn't the Ridgemont way. But instead, Mr. Hastings is asking the question that no one else has—*why?*

"I kind of feel like it should be obvious," she says. "I mean, you do know what happened in December? My 'challenging life changes'? She puts her last words in air quotes.

But Mr. Hastings keeps on going, still wearing an expression fresh out of a PowerPoint presentation titled "How to Connect with Emotionally Disturbed Minors."

"When a student like you begins to fail classes," he says, "and in her junior year no less, which is the most important year for college admissions, we really start to worry about her. We try to figure out how to help her. Emma, we are committed to supporting you. To seeing you through this difficult time. So I ask you, what can we do better?"

Once again, Hastings takes her by surprise. Sarcastically tossing his own words back didn't ruffle him at all. Emma would almost buy it, if every word out of his mouth wasn't corporatespeak.

"You can start by not pretending that your concern is

me," Emma says. "It's Ridgemont's reputation. What happens to the school's statistics if one of its students—like me—starts bringing down the collective GPA?"

"That's absolutely not true," Mr. Hastings says. "We care about all of our students. We particularly care about *you*."

"Mmmm…maybe it's more like you care about Byron Blake's daughter," Emma says doubtfully. She picks at a snag on the sleeve of her sweater.

"I understand that it might be difficult to concentrate on schoolwork right now. I understand that there are… extenuating circumstances," Mr. Hastings goes on.

"That's one way to put it," Emma says. The snag becomes a small hole.

"A death in the family is a terrible thing. And when it's so recent—well, I understand that you are deep, deep in the grieving process."

Anger floods Emma's body, a chewed fingernail catching on the hole in her sweater. "You can't even say the *word*," she says. "I'm going through 'challenging life changes,' with 'extenuating circumstances.' If you can't say the word, how can you possibly understand how I feel?"

Hastings closes his eyes. It looks to Emma like he's trying to gather his strength. Then his eyes open with a snap, and he stares right at her. *"Suicide,"* he says, "is the tragedy of the greatest proportions."

There. He said it. She didn't think he would. Mr. Hastings

keeps swinging at her pitches. And even though she made him do it, it still hits her like a gut punch.

"When people are grieving," Mr. Hastings goes on, "they sometimes have very dark thoughts. But these must remain *thoughts* only. I cannot have you going around talking about setting yourself on fire, Emma Blake. There are other ways to express your sadness. And there are far better ways to process it. Do you understand me?"

What Emma now understands is that Mr. Hastings doesn't think she's serious about actually doing it. He thinks she's having "thoughts only," as a mean to "express her sadness."

She's about to tell him how wrong he is when it occurs to her that his ignorance could be to her advantage. The less Mr. Hastings knows about her plans, the harder it will be for him to stop them.

CHAPTER 4

SO SHE NODS and says, "Yes. I understand you. I understand that you're trying to take away my right of free speech. Just like you did with the newspaper."

She crosses her arms, pleased with her deft shift in topic. Now Mr. Hastings will have to address the fact that she was the editor in chief of the *Ridgemont Trumpet* for four whole months before they censored her right out of it, mostly because of the word he struggled so hard to enunciate a few moments earlier.

But it's Mr. Montgomery who speaks first. "Emma, be reasonable," he says. "We couldn't have you writing upsetting things in the school paper."

"You mean you can't have me writing the truth," Emma says.

"It's very complicated," Mr. Hastings says.

"No," Emma says. "There's nothing simpler than the truth. The problem is that no one ever wants to hear it."

That's why she wrote the essay for Montgomery's class—to tell the truth. But they stopped her before she even got there. They got hung up on the gruesome details.

In a matter of seconds, blisters will erupt on my skin. My hair will ignite.

Okay, maybe she could've been a little more subtle. If she had, maybe she'd have gotten to the last line: *You*—all of you—*are sleepwalking through global catastrophe. And with my death, I intend to wake you up.*

"Emma," Mr. Hastings says, "we're worried about you. You are a brilliant student—a leader at Ridgemont. Please don't let all that slip away."

"Correction," Emma says. "I used to be a leader at Ridgemont. After I realized that everyone here walks around with blinders on, I decided I didn't want to lead sheep." The leather creaks as Emma gets up from her chair. "I can't believe my grades actually matter to you when the whole *world* is in crisis."

Mr. Hastings blinks at her in surprise. "We aren't talking about the world here, Emma—"

"Well, you should be! That's my entire point." Which they would know if they'd let her finish reading her essay.

"You're trying to distract us from the problem at hand,"

Mr. Hastings says, "which is your erratic and disturbing behavior."

Emma barks out a laugh. "If my behavior is what you think is 'the problem at hand,' you haven't read the news."

Mr. Hastings reaches down and extracts that day's *New York Times* from his recycling bin. He pushes the paper toward Emma so she can see the headlines: HUNDREDS FEARED DEAD AFTER MYANMAR FLOOD; THE HUMAN COST OF A BROKEN IMMIGRATION SYSTEM.

"I read the news every day," he says quietly. "But my job is to care for the students under my charge. Which is why I'm putting you on academic probation and making you an appointment to speak to the school counselor."

"And you'll rewrite your essay," Mr. Montgomery adds. "And it will be well crafted and *appropriate*, the way your essays were last semester. You are capable of it, and it will be good for you."

"It's a challenge you can rise to," Mr. Hastings agrees. "However, I will add that I do want our students to find their work fulfilling. Like Mr. Montgomery, I believe an appropriate topic is necessary, and I also believe that you can find one that you care about. It seems that global issues matter to you. Why not write about climate change? Or our failing health care system?"

Emma wants to scream. Everyone's so desperate for her to be the happy, active girl she used to be. She's been the freaking Ridgemont poster child, getting straight A's in her classes, leading student clubs, dominating on the soccer field and the tennis court. Everyone misses that girl terribly, and they'd do anything to get her back.

Hell, even Emma misses her. But she can't get her back.

That girl is gone forever. That girl died in December too.

"People already write about those things," Emma says quietly, tapping her fingernail on his copy of the *New York Times*. "No one is listening to scientists, to experts, to doctors and lawyers and people with a string of degrees after their names. No one is going to listen to a privileged white girl unless she does something drastic. I already rose to your challenges, and I accomplished nothing that actually mattered. I don't want to be your poster child anymore."

Mr. Hastings leans across his desk so his face is barely a foot away from hers. She can see the individual pores on his nose.

"But do you want to set yourself on fire?" he asks.

"Of course she doesn't!" Mr. Montgomery exclaims. "She just wanted to shock all of us!"

Emma's seen what Mr. Montgomery drives: a Honda Civic. His suit jackets are off-the-rack, not tailor-made. He probably eats the heels of his bread loaves, drinks Walmart coffee, and drives to school every day believing that none of his rich students have any real problems. *But we're living on the same planet, and the outlook is not good.*

Mr. Hastings, however, is still holding her gaze, still waiting for an answer to whether or not she actually wants to set herself on fire…and he looks like he might actually care about her response.

Emma swivels away from Mr. Hastings and offers Mr. Montgomery a half smile. "It was a good presentation, admit it," she tells him. "*Everyone* was paying attention. You can't say that about anyone else's essay. You could barely keep your eyes open during Rhaina's exploration of the joys of a French horn."

Mr. Montgomery stiffens. He looks like he's being strangled by his tie. "I won't tell you it was good."

Emma lifts an eyebrow, mildly surprised. Sure, she's failing English now, and most of her other classes. But she used to get A's in her sleep. "Okay, then," she says. "What grade would you give it?"

She tries to make it sound like she doesn't actually care all that much, but there's still a little bit of pride deep down, a tiny place inside of her that wants to know she could climb out of this hole she's dug for herself—if she really wanted to.

"Setting aside the issue of the topic and its utter inappropriateness for AP English," Mr. Montgomery says, "I'd give you a C plus. Maybe a B minus."

"That's it?" Emma is truly surprised.

Old Emma would have spent ten minutes before class

drafting essays, spouting clichés and well-worn phrases that she knew adults liked and would reward with A's. But she put real effort into today's essay, revealed in those pages her heart, soul, and core beliefs.

"The sentences were elegant," Mr. Montgomery goes on. "The details were awful but powerful. However, I asked for an essay that described your personal experience. Your essay came from *research*."

Dammit. The man is not wrong.

It's ironic, though, isn't it? In another few days, she actually *would* be able to write about burning from personal experience. Except for the whole problem of being dead.

"I understand your point," she says calmly. "I'll try to do better next time."

But if Emma gets her way—and she usually does—there won't be a next time.

CHAPTER 5

ALONE AGAIN FINALLY, Hastings wipes his brow with a spotless white handkerchief and then tosses it into the small brass bin beneath his desk. (He never uses a handkerchief more than once.)

He's troubled by the fact that in a matter of months, Emma Blake has gone from being one of Ridgemont's best students to one of its worst. She's going through a rough patch, but he believes it to be temporary. She'll turn herself around, because that's what Ridgemont students do. Especially when they have support from friends and family.

Of course, he must admit, family is part of the problem. Emma barely has a family anymore. And her father—the only one left—is the kind of person Hastings might call "problematic."

What's also problematic is the fact that Emma never actually answered his question. Does she really want to set herself on fire?

Mr. Montgomery would like to write off her behavior as youthful theatrics designed to create a stir and guarantee attention, but Hastings has been around teenagers his entire professional life—and Emma Blake doesn't need attention.

Emma is the kind of young person who makes adults feel like maybe the human race isn't barreling headfirst into a brick wall that's going to break its collective neck. Or at least she used to be.

Hastings long ago resigned himself to the fact that he would never be a father, but when Emma arrived at Ridgemont—smart, strong, deservedly proud, quick, and funny—he realized she was exactly the daughter he wishes he could have had. Instead, she's stuck with the biological father she actually got. One who can't be bothered.

"Fiona," he calls, steeling himself, "get Byron Blake on the line for me."

"Righto, righto," she chirps.

Emma's father is a prominent Boston attorney specializing in white-collar defense. His clients, almost exclusively CEOs and VIPs, are men like Hastings's cousin Charlie, who had to hire Blake to defend him against embezzlement charges.

"He costs fifteen hundred an hour, but he never loses," Charlie bragged. He was right too: Blake won the case, and Charlie avoided ten years in prison.

Hastings tries not to resent Charlie for risking a decade without his wife and children all for the sake of money. Meanwhile, Hastings has declined two raises in the past five years, asking instead that the funding go to mental health support for the students.

Students that he worries about, students who—no matter how well off they are—are data points on line charts that plot the skyrocketing anxiety and depression rates among teenagers. Students like Emma Blake. Students who have parents like Byron Blake, and his own cousin Charlie…parents who'd rather throw money at a problem than actually talk to their kids.

Throwing money around is a major pastime of Byron Blake's, and a lot of that money has landed at Ridgemont Academy.

A lot.

Hastings tries to slow his pulse as he listens to Fiona addressing Blake's assistant—"Yes, dear, it's important"—and then announcing, "All yours, Mr. Hastings." When he picks up the receiver, a suave British voice asks him to hold for Mr. Blake, and then Blake tersely says, "Yes."

The word is a simple statement letting Hastings know that he's there.

"Good morning, Mr. Blake. This is Perry Hastings from Ridge—"

"I'm aware. What is this about?"

"It concerns your daughter, Emma," Hastings says, maintaining his composure in the face of Blake's obvious impatience. "I'm calling because she read a disturbing piece in her English class today. It was very upsetting to everyone."

"What was it about?" Blake asks, but Hastings can hear typing in the background, Blake's only surviving daughter's disturbing behavior relegated to multitasking.

"She announced her intention to set herself on fire." Hastings is pleased when the sound of typing comes to an abrupt halt.

There is silence on the other end of the line. Finally, Blake says, "And?"

"Well, sir," Hastings says, "I thought you should be alerted. It strikes me as a red flag." More like a red tapestry, one woven with blood, fire, and the spark of determination he saw in Emma's eyes.

When Byron merely grunts, Hastings is forced to stumble on. "Though we're confident we can keep Emma safe," he says, "we are concerned about her current mental state. Apparently she went into great detail about what burning would be like."

But Hastings isn't confident, not at all. He's seen Emma finish a soccer match with one eye swollen shut. She wasn't bleeding, she reasoned, refusing to be benched. The coach—probably thinking of the brand-new jerseys recently gifted from the Blake Corporation—let her continue to play, and she scored the winning goal, with only half her vision intact.

When Emma Blake makes a decision, it is irreversible.

"What was the assignment?" Blake demands.

Hastings feels a trickle of sweat slide down his neck. "It was a descriptive essay."

"Was there an assigned topic?"

"No, but—"

"Were there forbidden topics?"

"I'm not certain about that—"

"You should've been clear before you called me. It's called gathering evidence."

"With all due respect, sir," Hastings says, "whether or not her teacher listed forbidden topics, Emma's essay is cause for concern—"

"But she wasn't told that she couldn't write about setting herself on fire."

"I don't believe so, but—"

"Obviously it'd make for a gripping essay. I'll bet you could've heard a pin drop in that room."

Hastings glances down at Emma's essay, which Mr. Montgomery left on his desk. *When exposed to heat, the muscles in my thighs will shrink and retract along the shafts of my femur…*

He shudders, feels a cold wave move over his body, despite the sheen of sweat that a phone call with Bryon always causes. How can a man who has handled some of the biggest legal cases in the country be missing the point so entirely?

"I apologize, sir," he said, "but regardless of the parameters of the assignment or how riveting the presentation may have been, what I'm concerned about here is the intent behind Emma's essay. Especially in light of the present circumstances and her situation—"

"Which circumstances exactly?"

Hastings can't bring himself to speak of the deaths in the Blake family. He doesn't want to say "cancer." He already said "suicide" once. Why must everyone in the Blake family be so intent on making others uncomfortable?

"Emma's grades have been slipping," he finally says, trying to steer the conversation toward something Byron might actually care about—winning.

"She's the smartest one you've got at that school," Blake says, and Hastings can hear the pride in his voice.

"Emma is extremely intelligent, yes. But if she doesn't do the work, she doesn't get the grade."

"It sounds to me like she's doing the work, but you WASPy graspers don't approve of it."

"Now Mr. Blake, let's be civil—"

"This *is* me being civil."

Hastings sighs. Without thinking, he glances down at Emma's essay again.

During the burning, my muscles will contract, and this will cause my joints to flex. My hands may pull up into a boxer's pose...

"English is not the only area of concern, frankly," Hastings says. "But much more important than Emma's GPA is her mental health."

My bones will survive the fire when all other soft tissues have burned away. But they will likely exhibit U-shaped fractures...

"Emma's fine. She's strong. Steady," Blake insists.

"She's strong, yes, of course, but even strong people get tired. Right now she may need some extra support." Hastings stares out the window at the green lawn, now dotted with students eating lunch. Emma isn't among them. "We think it would be best if you could come to the school tomorrow. Maybe check in with her. Take her out to dinner. Have some family time."

Have what's-left-of-your-family time, he adds silently.

"I'm in the middle of a trial," Blake says. "It's a huge case. Lives are at stake."

Hastings isn't bold enough to suggest that a life might be at stake here too, but what Byron said about his own daughter is exactly the problem. She is steady. And she's clearly set her course.

"Sir," he says, "Ridgemont cares deeply about its student body. Exceptional students like Emma—"

"Spare me," Blake says. "I lip-service my clients all day, I know what bullshit smells like—and sounds like."

Bullshit. This man's daughter has announced her intention to set herself on fire, and he wants to argue with Hastings about whether or not *Hastings* actually cares about Emma.

"Sir," Hastings tries again, not ready to give up quite yet, even if he is irritating their largest donor. "The pressure to do well can be overwhelming, especially when one is struggling with—"

"It was schoolwork. Nothing more than that. Emma was just pushing the envelope. That's what she does. That's what I taught her to do."

And with that, Blake hangs up.

CHAPTER 6

EMMA PACES BACK and forth across a square of moonlight on the dorm room floor. It's past midnight. She barely paid attention in her last class of the day, Philosophy and Ethics, but a line from the philosopher Arthur Schopenhauer is stuck in her head anyway. "Every person takes the limits of their own field of vision for the limits of the world," he wrote.

Emma's interpretation of this is simple: If a person can't picture something happening in their mind, they think that it can't actually happen in real life.

That person would be wrong, of course, and Emma is living proof of it. She'd never imagined a world where she lost her family like dominoes, one after the other. But here she is.

Twelve steps to the east wall, twelve steps back to the west. Emma's probably walked a mile just inside her dorm room tonight, while her roommate, Olivia, snores under a flowered comforter. Olivia hasn't heard anything about Emma's essay yet, and Emma hasn't told her about getting marched into Hastings's office.

If Emma couldn't imagine things happening in real life, Olivia is an example of someone who can't distinguish between her real life and her online one. The whole campus is buzzing about Emma's morning exploits, but Olivia's most important contacts aren't on campus—they are her followers and subscribers across Instagram, TikTok, and YouTube, all feeders for her OnlyFans, which she says she's only doing in order to be able to afford Yale.

If Olivia isn't studying, she's building her brand, expanding her audience, and analyzing algorithms. Meanwhile, Emma googles "climate crisis" and "teen mental health" and "modern day slavery" and "five stages of grief" and then writes essays about self-immolation. It's possible they aren't the best fit.

She peels off her socks and tosses them into the corner. Sinks into her uncomfortable desk chair. She's never going to be able to sleep. She wishes she could blame Olivia's snoring, but it's Emma's own brain that's the problem. Thoughts swirling with nowhere to go. Words waiting in her throat. It's bad in the day, but it's gotten intolerable at night.

If only I could call Claire.

She's *still* pissed she never got to finish reading her essay out loud. But not because she wants the good grade she thinks she deserves. An A doesn't matter when you're dead. But if she can make her death matter, she'll call that a win.

CHAPTER 7

WHEN OLIVIA MAKES a particularly violent snort, Emma considers the fact that posting a pic of her roommate in her CPAP mask could ruin her online identity as a sex object. Just the other day, Olivia surpassed ten thousand followers on her Instagram, and she shrieked that information at Emma, who was working on the part of her essay where she described the wicking effect of her body fat melting. She finds Olivia's goals immature, but she can't deny that the girl has an audience. Which gives her an idea.

Emma grabs her phone and sneaks down the hall. She tiptoes past the dorm monitor's room, since Mrs. Vickers has hearing so sharp it's like she's bugged the hall with microphones. Once she's safely on the other side, she breaks into a soft jog. Passes the bathroom and the janitor's closet. Hangs a right into the student lounge.

Lights out was two hours ago, so the lounge is dark and empty. But it still smells like microwaved popcorn, and Emma's stomach rumbles. She skipped dinner again. She didn't want to be ambushed by people asking about her essay. Plus food doesn't taste as good as it used to. She brushes aside a memory of visiting Claire in New York—Claire holding up a foot-long Coney dog, begging Emma to dig in on the other end and see who got to the middle first. They ended up with noses touching, Coney sauce dripping off their chins, laughing.

She sinks into the cushions on a big soft couch and props her feet up on the battered coffee table. She holds the phone to her face and opens the camera. Selfie mode. Video.

She pushes her bangs off her forehead, but they slide right back into place. In early January, Emma cut off her hair. Just walked into the bathroom with a pair of kitchen scissors and chopped off eighteen inches in two giant snips. Now she has a black bob, one side longer than the other. People say she looks like Uma Thurman in *Pulp Fiction,* but Emma hasn't watched the movie to see if they're right.

She takes a deep breath. Her palms feel damp. She wipes them impatiently on her sweatpants. Wonders when she became the kind of person who has sweaty hands.

Maybe it was about the same time she became the kind of person who plans her own death.

She tries one more time to brush her bangs aside. It doesn't work. She presses the red button with her fingertip and looks right into the camera as she talks. Her voice comes out shaky at first. Quiet, too, but that's on purpose. That's because of Mrs. Vickers and her bat ears.

"Hey, guys," she says. "I don't know who's out there. Who's going to see this. But I have something to say, and I hope there are a few of you out there who want to listen. My name's Emma. I'm seventeen years old. And today in class I read an essay about burning myself alive." She smiles nervously. "Well, I read *part* of an essay about burning myself alive. I didn't get to finish it, because my teacher freaked out. Go figure."

Emma shuts her eyes for a second to gather her thoughts, then opens them again and goes on. "I got to talk a lot about what happens to a burning body, which is—well, it's gross. But there was a lot that I didn't get to say. For instance, I didn't get to say *why*. So I'm going to tell you why I'm going to do it."

She stops for moment, listening. The lounge is still silent. She's still safe. "I should add that if just killing myself was the only goal, I could find a nicer way to do it. Although maybe *nicer*'s not the word. Maybe I just mean less terrible. Fire is literally the worst possible way to go. But that's why it makes such a powerful statement."

She pushes her hair back again. "And I want to make a

statement about the state of our world. Do you understand how dark our future looks? No, you don't. You're not paying attention. You're in denial. *All of you out there are sleepwalking through a global catastrophe.* A whole bunch of catastrophes, honestly. But when I light that flame, you're going to wake up. You're going to start paying attention."

"Emma?"

Emma twists around, heart pounding. Silhouetted against the light of the hallway is Mrs. Vickers, hair piled in a gravity-defying bun on the top of her head and huge fuzzy slippers on her feet. Emma quickly hits STOP and slips her phone into her pocket.

"Um, hi, Mrs. V," she says. "Sorry, I couldn't sleep."

"But what are you doing out here in the dark?" Mrs. Vickers demands. "Were you talking to someone? Is anyone else up?" She flicks the switch, and the lounge explodes with light. She sniffs. "Were you using the microwave?"

Emma squints against the brightness. "It's just me," she says. "I wasn't using the microwave."

"All students must be in their rooms after lights out," Mrs. Vickers says, not unkindly. "If they lie on their beds burning their eyes and boiling their brains on their phones, I can't exactly stop it." She taps a fuzzy-slippered foot on the shiny oak floor, eyeing Emma's pajama-pants pocket, and the obvious bulge of her phone there. "Hustle back to where you belong, please."

Emma pushes herself up from the couch. "Sorry, Mrs. V," she whispers.

She tries to slink past Mrs. Vickers and scurry back to her room, but the old woman is too quick. She catches Emma's sleeve in her grip.

"Oh, my dear," she says, her voice now thick with sorrow, "I think about you, you know. I just can't get over what happened to your sister. She lived in the room next to yours. She was the loveliest girl I ever saw."

Emma ducks her head. "I know, you've told me," she says softly. *Like five hundred times.*

"If you ever need anything, you come to me, do you hear? Just make sure it's before lights out." Mrs. Vickers winks. Then she actually pinches Emma's cheek, like she's a little kid. "Good night, child," she says. "Sleep tight."

Maybe it should feel good, maybe Emma should be grateful. Instead what she feels is an adult trying to replace her mother—who would never, ever have pinched her cheek and told her to sleep tight. Maybe tapped her shoulder and told her not to let the bedbugs bite—and if they did, to definitely let her know, because that meant the cleaning staff needed to be fired.

"Yes, ma'am," Emma says. "Good night."

When she gets back to her room, Olivia is still snoring. Emma opens her phone. Clicks on the photos app. When her video comes up, she almost presses PLAY.

But she's afraid that if she watches it, she might lose her nerve. So with a couple of clicks, she labels the file "Fire Video #1, EMMA" and uploads it to YouTube. She decides she won't check the comments right away.

forest man *2 hours ago*

fight your demons, you are strong I believe in you 💪💪🙏🙏

jakob23456 *3 hours ago*

i wuld watch her Burn

Alicelovescats *3 hours ago*

don't do it—know that ur important, ur amazing just the way you are

sophia allemande *4 hours ago*

the thing about cutting is that you get a sick thrill out of seeing your blood but burning just sux

Ash *5 hours ago*

WTF is this bitch serious?

CHAPTER 8

Three days before the fire

EMMA FINALLY FALLS asleep at four in the morning. Sometime around seven, she turns off her blaring alarm. By the time she gets up, breakfast is over, and she has ten minutes to get to class on time.

She dresses quickly, runs a brush through her hair, and manages to make it into Ridgemont's brand-new, state-of-the-art chemistry classroom a minute before the bell rings. She slides into her seat, stomach rumbling. She offers Ava Green, who is flat-out staring at her, a half smile.

Ava just blinks at her.

"Are you, like, okay?" she whispers.

Emma shrugs. She doesn't even know how to answer

the question. If your mood only ranges from pitch-black to dull gray, what qualifies as "like, okay"? Is now the right time to explain what chiaroscuro is?

Also, does Ava actually care how she feels?

"I heard about your essay," Ava says. "You weren't serious, were you?"

No, of course Ava does not actually care how Emma feels. Ava is not concerned so much as *curious*. To her—and to most of Ridgemont—Emma is not a person; she is a curiosity. A rich, pretty, white girl who isn't flourishing, and no one can understand why a person with all of her advantages in life isn't performing up to standard.

Ava Green practically is the standard. Ava's one of the Ridgemont princesses, a shiny-haired girl from Connecticut whose primary interests are boys and gossip. And at the moment, Emma is good gossip.

Emma shrugs again. "I don't know," she says. She opens her notebook and starts pretending to look over her notes so Ava will leave her alone.

Ava takes the hint and turns to her other neighbor. "Did you hear about that insane essay Emma wrote?" she asks Eden Graham in a stage whisper.

"No! Tell me!"

Thankfully the bell rings and their teacher starts talking, which drowns out whatever Ava has to say about Emma's self-immolation essay. Although other people are probably talking about it, too, Emma realizes—they just aren't doing it right in front of her face.

She wonders if anyone's seen the video. Probably not. Certainly there wouldn't be many Ridgemont students checking YouTube before breakfast. Their GPAs, though, maybe. Olivia reaches for her phone as soon as she wakes up in order to plot her data points on her follower graph, but Emma has never seen the allure.

"—so make your way back to the lab tables," Ms. Geller is saying. "Partners are the same as last week." Her tone turns threatening. "Cormac, if I see that phone in your hand again, I'm going to drop it in sulfuric acid."

"Chemical formula H_2SO_4," adds Simon, the teacher's pet.

At Emma's lab station, Elliott Jameson, her partner and Ridgemont's star quarterback, says, "Morning, gorgeous."

"Morning, meathead." Emma does her best to offer him a real smile. She actually likes Elliott, even if he's never read a book he wasn't forced to. He has big blue eyes and Cupid curls; he looks like a grown-up baby doll. She surreptitiously checks for a pull string in his back, and wonders if "Morning, gorgeous" is one of his preloaded statements.

"Directions are in the packet at your stations," Ms. Geller says. "I know that I don't need to tell you this, but open flames are dangerous, so please be careful with your precious limbs."

"Ha ha, don't get any crazy fire ideas, Emma," Spencer Jenkins calls from the neighboring table.

Emma rolls her eyes at him. Spencer thinks he's funny because no one has ever told him he isn't. Probably no one has told him no in his whole life either. For his sixteenth birthday he got a custom Rivian with $100,000 in the glove compartment. Ava sniffed and called him nouveau riche, but Spencer just grinned and said, "The *riche* is all that matters, baby." And maybe that was what it took to convince her, because two weeks later, they were stuck together like lampreys outside the student union.

Emma can't stand either of them anymore. But is it really their fault? Or is it because now she envies them? Not because they're rich—Emma comes from money too—but because nothing bad has ever happened to them.

She watches as Ava blows Spencer a kiss. Probably it's a little bit of both.

"Dude," Elliott says. "Earth to Planet Emma."

Emma jumps. "Sorry," she says. She opens the lab packet and turns to the right page. She's so tired that the words blur and seem to dance. " 'Before you begin,' " she manages to read, " 'ensure that you are wearing appropriate safety gear, including safety goggles.' "

Elliott hands her a pair, and she slips them on. He's wearing a lab coat now, too, so suddenly he looks like a grown-up baby doll who dressed as a mad scientist for Halloween.

" 'Dip the Nichrome loop into the beaker containing hydrochloric acid to moisten the loop,' " Emma goes on.

"'Then dip the loop into the beaker holding the strontium nitrate. Ignite the Bunsen burner.'"

Elliott dips the wire into the right beakers and hands it to Emma while he lights the burner. It makes a low hissing sound; the flame burns steady and pale blue.

When Emma holds the treated wire loop in the Bunsen's flame, it turns a brilliant red.

"Dude," Elliott says, because *dude* is his favorite word. "Totally satanic."

"Don't write that in the notebook," Emma says. "Just put 'red.'" She cleans the loop, dips it into the next beaker, and offers it to Elliott. "Your turn."

The barium chloride burns apple green at the end of the loop. Emma writes this down.

"I should also not need to remind you to make your observations *legible*," Ms. Geller calls. "Maria, Spencer, James—I'm looking at you three in particular."

Emma's eyes wander off the lab paper, the flickering light of the flame drawing her in. How hot is it? A couple thousand degrees?

Elliott says, "Okay, what does it say we're supposed to do next?"

Emma doesn't answer. Why does it matter what compound they test? It's a stupid experiment. They could simply write down a series of colors and pass this lab.

Or they could google all the answers in two seconds.

Which Cormac is probably doing with the phone he's not supposed to have in class. He, like Emma, knows this is sixth-grade science. But—as Ava pointed out with a sniff when she googled Ms. Geller—their new teacher came to them from a public school. Ava practically sneered the words, shocked that somehow she'd be receiving instruction from someone who had been moving among the general public only months earlier.

"Ugh," Elliott says, "where are the directions—hang on—"

Emma hears him, sort of. But her attention is focused on the steady gas flame. And on her arm moving toward it.

How can she explain what she does next?

Call it an experiment.

Or maybe a test.

She holds her arm three inches above the Bunsen burner's flame. It doesn't hurt right away. At first she feels nothing but warmth. But then the pain comes, and it does so in a white-hot rush, and suddenly it's so bad that her brain starts to short-circuit.

One second. A knife made of fire pushes into her skin.

Two seconds. The blade is twisting inside her arm, cutting muscles as it spins. She isn't Emma Blake anymore. She's nothing but pain.

Three seconds. Shredding tendons. Splintering bone. The sun burning inside her skin.

Four seconds. It isn't heat. It's *agony.*

"Whoa, what the fuck!" Elliott shouts. He knocks her arm away and the burner tips over, the flames shooting sideways. A lab notebook ignites.

People are yelling now. Emma's vision swims, her brain now processing more than just pain. There's a red welt on her arm...and the smell of burning flesh. Why didn't she include what it would smell like in her descriptive essay?

"Stand back!" Ms. Geller's shouting. "Stand back!" The fire extinguisher sends out a white chemical stream.

Emma falls to her knees. Clutches her wrist, inches from the burn. The first moments away from the flame are somehow even worse. The pain radiates up her forearm. Now it's in her shoulder. The side of her face. It feels like she's pressing her skin against a supernova. She feels sick to her stomach. She grabs the edge of the lab table with her good hand. Tries to stand up. Bile rises in her throat.

"Jesus, Emma, are you okay? What were you doing?" Elliott's voice sounds panicked. High and girlish.

Ms. Geller runs over, her face white as paper. Emma holds her arm like she's trying to hide it from her. The class is in an uproar.

I did it, Emma tells herself. *Now I know what it feels like.*

CHAPTER 9

EMMA GETS TAKEN to the headmaster's office for the second time in two days. She'd be angry about this if she could feel anything at all besides pain.

Idiot, you shouldn't have done it, part of her says.

I had to, says another part. *I needed to know.*

But you didn't need to do it in the middle of class.

"Emma," Mr. Hastings says, his voice thick with concern, "first an essay about burning—now an actual burn. What on earth happened in chemistry this morning?"

She blinks at the headmaster. Yes, if she had thought things through a little better, then she wouldn't be sitting in a stuffy office, facing a balding man in a three-piece suit who's looking at her like she's gone absolutely crazy. But there's more in his eyes than there was in Mr. Montgomery's, who was clearly more worried about the effect of the fall-out on his career than about Emma's physical safety. And Ms. Geller didn't know whom to care for first—Emma or the classroom full of billionaires' children who just got their first shot of real trauma.

Emma presses her lips together. She'd like to cross her arms defiantly, but she can't let the burn touch anything. The nurse, Mrs. Ereckson, has cleaned and bandaged it and given her two Tylenol and two Advil all at once. But her arm still feels like it's actually on fire. The pain is nearly unbearable. It hurts so bad she can't imagine it ever stopping. Which raises the question of whether Emma will be able to follow through when the time comes to make her final, unequivocal point.

"Bunsen burners are dangerous things," Emma says, keeping her voice noncommittal.

"Yes, they are. You nearly set an entire classroom on fire," Mr. Hastings says. "But that's beside the point, believe it or not."

"It was actually Elliott who knocked it over," Emma says. "If you care."

Mr. Hastings's glance darkens. "It's my understanding that he knocked it over in an attempt to stop you from holding your arm over the flame." He sighs and rubs one pale, bushy eyebrow. "You're not here because you're in trouble, Emma. You're here because I'm truly, truly worried about you. You led me to believe that your essay was a thought experiment. But self-harm is different. It's an extremely dangerous thing."

"No," Emma says thoughtfully, tilting her head to one side. "I didn't lead you to believe my essay was a thought experiment. You chose to believe that for your own comfort."

Mr. Hastings's mouth falls open, a flicker of something Emma can't quite decipher passing over his eyes.

At that moment the door swings open, and Fiona Dundy comes in, bearing a tray with two blue china cups, which she sets down in front of them.

"You're worried about me, so you invited me to a tea party?" Emma asks Mr. Hastings dryly.

"It's coffee, dear," Fiona chirps. "You look so tired! And Mr. Hastings drinks the stuff like it's water."

"If you'll excuse us, Fiona," Mr. Hastings says through clenched teeth—which, yes, Emma can now see do show distinct signs of coffee stains. Interesting that he doesn't shell out for teeth whitening. Fiona is still hovering, waiting for Emma to take a sip.

Dutifully, Emma picks up the delicate cup, using her good arm. The coffee tastes like ashes. "Delicious," she says, "thank you," and Fiona beams at her before hurrying back to her desk.

When the door closes behind her, Mr. Hastings trains

his gaze on Emma again. "I must assume there's a direct connection between writing an essay about burning yourself and then actually burning yourself," he says.

He's a regular Sherlock Holmes, isn't he? But Emma keeps her mouth shut.

"And as I was saying, self-harm is a very serious issue."

"It wasn't really self-harm," Emma says.

"No?"

"It was an experiment."

Mr. Hastings frowns. "Are you trying to tell me that you hurt yourself during a science experiment by mistake?"

It's obvious that he wants this to be true, just like he wanted her essay to be simply a thought experiment. The problem, of course, is that it isn't.

"Hurting myself was a side effect of the experiment," Emma says. It's a sentence that's open to interpretation.

Mr. Hastings takes a large gulp of coffee, emptying his cup in one practiced flick of his wrist. "I don't understand."

For a second, Emma is torn. It'd make the next few days of her life—the *last* few days of her life—so much easier if she just lied to him. If she pretended it was all a mistake, and that everything was all right.

But people pretending that everything is all right is exactly why *the whole entire world* is such a mess. It's the reason she wrote her essay in the first place. So, no, she can't lie to him. As much as she wants to.

"What I mean is," she says, very slowly, "the experiment was about measuring how long I could hold my arm over a flame."

Mr. Hastings pales, his fingers tightening on the delicate handle of the teacup.

"Getting a third-degree burn was a side effect," Emma says. "Or a *result*, you might even say."

"Oh, Emma," he whispers. He honestly looks like he's about to cry. He sets the teacup down on the desk, his elbows following quickly after, his head falling forward into his hands.

She watches his fingers dig through what's left of his salt-and-pepper hair, noticing the flesh puffing on either side of his wedding ring. Mr. Hastings has clearly gained weight during his marriage, as Emma has read that people in healthy relationships tend to do. It's odd to think about Mr. Hastings as a real person, going home to his wife, but for some reason she does hope he's happy.

She turns away and gazes out the window. Two little brown birds keep flying in and out of the bush outside the headmaster's office. They're building a nest for their eggs. She imagines little fluffy, dust-colored chicks peeping, crying out to be fed.

Mr. Hastings pulls his face out of his hands. "I'm calling your father right now."

She assumes sparrows aren't the world's most loving

parents. But at least the dad bird won't always be flying off to his law office. And probably the mom bird won't die of cancer. Or maybe she will. Emma is sure there's a study out there somewhere stating that birds are dying of just about everything, because humans are such absolute pieces of shit.

"Emma?" Her dad's gruff voice comes through Hastings's speakerphone. "What is going on?"

Emma sighs. "Hi, Dad. How's trial?"

"We're not talking about me, Emma, we're talking about you, and why I'm getting another call from your school."

As usual, there's a tone to his voice that doesn't quite fit his words. Yes, he wants to insist that they're talking about her and not him, but the annoyance level she's detecting tells her that talking about her *at all* isn't a priority right now. Or probably ever.

"Everyone's overreacting again," Emma says.

"To what?"

"I burned myself in science class."

He waits a beat. "On purpose," he says. It's not a question.

"Yes."

"Why?"

"I wanted to see if I could take it."

It's not exactly what she said to Hastings, and it clearly hits him hard. He gets up from his chair, loosens his tie, walks over to the window. She hopes he's watching the sparrows, hopes that he can give his attention to something that actually matters right now, and not this charade of a family phone call.

Her father grunts. She can picture him now: tailor-made suit, Brioni tie, salt-and-pepper hair perfectly combed. He's pacing his huge, light-filled office, because Byron Blake doesn't sit still. Doesn't suffer fools. And definitely doesn't want his daughter causing trouble at her exclusive high school. And yet—Byron has a touch of chaos in him, just like Emma does. A rebellious streak. He doesn't like to play by the rules.

"And could you?" he asks. "Take it?"

"Of course," Emma says flatly. "You know what you always used to tell us, Dad."

Then they say it together: "'Pain is weakness leaving the body.'"

At the window, Mr. Hastings puts his head against the glass, a deep exhalation fogging up the pane.

She remembers Sunday bike rides back when they were kids, their father goading them up hill after impossible hill with that very same phrase, the muscles in her legs burning, her sister pumping along beside her, sharing a glance of mutual misery while also being aware that whoever won would get the bigger ice-cream cone.

"But why did you do it?" her father asks.

Emma answers with a quote. "'Knowing yourself is the beginning of all wisdom.'"

"That's Aristotle," says her dad.

"You used to tell us that all the time too." *You've always borrowed other people's lines.* Parenting through quotes. He probably has a Pinterest board.

Hastings undoes his tie completely, pulling it away from his neck in one sharp movement. Clearly this phone call isn't going the way he thought it would at all.

"So you learned that you're tough," Byron Blake says.

Emma feels a surge of defiant pride. "Yes."

Her dad grunts again, but it almost sounds like a laugh. "But we already knew that," he says. "Your experiment was unnecessary."

Mr. Hastings finally manages to get his vocal cords working. "Sir," he says, "this isn't something we should be proud of. This is something we're deeply concerned about."

"How bad did it hurt?" her dad asks, as if he hasn't heard a single word Hastings said.

Emma clutches the underside of her injured arm. It hurts so much that sometimes it's hard to breathe. She wonders if it would hurt less now if she had burned it for longer. If she'd killed the nerves that caused the pain. That's what her research said was supposed to happen.

"The results of Emma's so-called experiment should not be the focus," Hastings says. "We need—we all need—to be asking why she did it, and what we can do collectively to support her and ensure it won't happen again."

"Searing pain," Emma says, following her dad's lead on ignoring the headmaster. "It felt like someone was pressing a sword through my arm, but the sword was made of red-hot lava. I could feel it in my teeth. My stomach. I thought I was going to throw up." She looks down at her bandage. "Now my arm is throbbing. It feels like I'm still being burned. Like it's still over the flame. I took Advil, but—"

"That's enough!" Mr. Hastings practically shouts. "Mr. Blake, we are seriously concerned about your daughter! I'm not sure you understand the gravity of the situation!"

"Emma, promise the man you won't do anything like this again." Her dad sounds bored, and she knows well enough the value of promises. How many trips to the zoo canceled at the last minute? Beach vacations for four suddenly reduced to three? Promises in the Blake family are simply words that you say. They don't have to carry any meaning or weight.

Emma chews her lip. She doesn't want to promise Hastings anything, doesn't want to follow the family pattern. But it's the quickest way to get out of this. "I, Emma Caroline Blake, solemnly swear not to burn myself in science class."

"Again," Hastings adds.

"And?" her dad presses.

"And I'll try harder at school. Bring up my GPA." *Blah blah blah.*

She sneaks another glance at the sparrows. One of them's perched on a branch with a fat, disgusting caterpillar in its mouth.

"That's my girl," her dad says. "You are the best of the best, Emma Caroline Blake. Don't let anyone forget that. Including yourself. I'll call you tomorrow."

Click.

Emma clutches her arm, right above the burn. As much as it hurts now, soon it'll be nothing but a scab, if she's alive long enough to finish the process. The body heals so much faster than the heart.

CHAPTER 10

Ava: did u hear about emma

Beatrix: ya that essay

Ava: no, in science she burned her arm on purpose

Ava: i was there

Beatrix: 😱😱😱 is she ok???

Ava: idk

Ava: she's crazy

Beatrix: that's mean

Ava: it's fact

Beatrix: she's had family tragedies

Ava: honestly she's always been a lunatic

Beatrix: ????

Ava: her whole family was nuts

Beatrix: stop
Ava: just sayin

Beatrix: u heard about emma?
Celia: y
Beatrix: have u talked to her
Celia: not yet
Beatrix: r u going to?
Celia: gonna tonight
Beatrix: give her a hug for me
Celia: 👍

Celia: we gotta go see emma 2night
Jade: bollocks i have to study
Celia: u don't know?
Jade: know what
Celia: she's saying she's going to set herself on fire
Jade: omfg
Celia: ikr
Celia: and she actually burned herself
Jade: guess im gonna fail my french test
Celia: come to my room at 7
Jade: k
Celia: ❤️

CHAPTER 11

AFTER HASTINGS LETS her go, Emma wanders over to the humanities building instead of going to her next class. Edgar Ridgemont, the school's founder, scowls down at her from his gold-framed portrait in the main hallway. Next to him, in a smaller portrait, is his wife, Lucinda, whose family money built the school, though she never got any credit for it. She also couldn't even send her own children to Ridgemont, because she had three daughters, and the school didn't accept girls until 1975.

Emma scowls back at Edgar Ridgemont, holding her hurt arm away from her body. She can feel the pain all the way from her shoulder deep down into her stomach, even though the actual burn is just a hot, blistery circle on her forearm, in the middle, between her wrist and her elbow. Taking a shower is going to be excruciating.

She knows she ought to go to her next class, but what's the point when she's already failing? What's the point of anything? Why does a diploma matter in a world that is falling apart?

She watches two students taping a poster on the wall next to Triple R, which is what everyone calls the Ridgemont Reading Room, a place where kids can study if they don't want to be in their rooms or the library. Triple R has vending machines and computer terminals and drawers full of school supplies for the taking, but Emma never goes inside anymore. It's try-hard territory. It's where students with long-term goals go. Emma's one goal is decidedly short-term.

The poster, she sees, is hand-painted—a sloppy picture of Earth underneath a smiling sun. HAPPY EARTH DAY, it reads. LOVE YOUR MOTHER.

Emma snorts. One of the students, a freckled freshman, turns around.

"Great poster," Emma says. "Way to stand up to Big Oil."

He looks at her in confusion.

"Earth Day!" she says. "I mean, seriously? As if paying attention to the planet once every three hundred sixty-five days could ever make any kind of difference. But really, I do like the painting. The sun's very nice."

Before he can answer, she walks away, heading toward the nearest open classroom door. A teacher whose name she doesn't know is lecturing a roomful of wide-eyed ninth graders. "Now the twenty-two letters of the Phoenician alphabet are basically simplified versions of Egyptian hieroglyphic symbols," he's saying. "But does anyone want to guess what the Phoenician alphabet was missing?"

Silence. Then two tentative hands get raised.

"Vowels," Emma says from the hallway. "The Phoenician alphabet didn't have vowels. Like Hebrew." Everyone turns to look at her. "You know—A, E, I, O, U." She pokes her head into the room. "*A* is for animal species, thousands of which are threatened with extinction due to climate change."

"Can I help you?" the teacher asks, walking toward her with a concerned look on his face.

"I don't know, can you? *E* is for emergency, as in 'We are in a climate emergency.' *I* is for the ice in the Arctic, which is melting a hell of a lot faster than anyone ever thought it would."

The teacher says, "This is extremely disruptive. Go find your own classroom." And he shuts the door in her face, after taking a quick glance up and down the hallway, as if expecting to see white-robed orderlies coming after her with syringes.

Emma turns away. Raises her voice, backpedaling as she moves away from the classroom. "*O* is for our oceans, which are becoming more and more acidic because they're absorbing so much of our excess carbon dioxide." She knocks her fist against the wall as she walks, dragging down the Earth Day poster. "That's only one of their problems, though. They're also getting too warm, and we're totally overfishing them. And hey, let's not forget that giant garbage patch of microplastics in the Pacific."

She passes open doors, catching glimpses of classes, students craning their necks to see what's going on out in the hallway. "*U*—what should *U* stand for? Oh, I know—how about *underwater*? Sea levels on the East Coast will rise a foot in the next thirty years. That should be fun!"

The bell rings. Students stream into the halls. They glance at her, then away when recognition sets in. It's just Emma Blake, breaking down again, making a scene. If only they would realize she's not trying to gain their attention for herself—it's for the world. Ultimately, it's for *them*.

"That takes care of our major vowels," Emma says, walking among them, raising her voice so people can hear her over the din. "So let's do consonants! Gotta back up to *B*, of course. *B* is for burning fossil fuels, which is what got us into this mess."

Most kids elbow past her, some giving her a wide berth, like they might catch her crazy. But Emma isn't daunted; there is method to her madness. Her voice gathers power. She sees a boy with floppy brown skater hair stop to listen.

"*C* is for the carbon emissions that come from burning these fossil fuels. *C* is also for Celsius. Earth's temperature has increased by almost one point two degrees Celsius in the last hundred and fifty years. Once we hit one point five degrees, *C* is for all the coral reefs that'll die."

"What is she talking about?" someone behind her asks. Not "What the hell is wrong with her?" Maybe she's getting through, gaining a foothold.

"Floods and droughts both become more frequent," Emma goes on. "Lightning strikes will increase! It'll mess up your daddies' golf games. Do you think that'll make them pay attention to the earth?"

She feels a hand on her arm. "Emma."

She shakes it off. "Where are we? *D*. Let's see—"

"Emma."

She's pulled all the way around, and now she's facing Rhaina Johnson, the uber-nerd from her English class. They've probably never said one word to each other before, but Rhaina is gripping her now by the shoulders and looking straight into Emma's eyes.

"Hey," Emma says wryly. "If you give me a second, I can get to *F*. I'll try to find a way to get French horns into the climate crisis."

"Are you drunk?" Rhaina demands. Her cheeks are pink, and her yellow hair is escaping from its double French braids.

"Of course not," Emma says. "I feel a little weird, though. Can you OD on Advil?"

"Okay, are you having a breakdown or something?" Rhaina blinks up at Emma, who's three inches taller at least.

Emma shakes her head side to side. Nope, no breakdown here!

Spencer walks past, staring at them. Ava, hurrying to catch up with him, widens her eyes in their direction.

"Hey, babygirl," Emma says, and Ava's eyes look like they might pop out of her head. "Your hair looks fantastic, by the way. Do me a favor and recycle that two-hundred-dollar shampoo bottle, okay?"

"What the hell are you doing?" Rhaina asks.

Emma brings her attention back to Rhaina. "Why do you care?"

"You're acting really weird!"

"What does that have to do with you?"

Rhaina is visibly sweating. She's watching everyone else watching them, and she clearly isn't enjoying it. Emma, on the other hand, feels lighter than she has in days. *What's a good fact for the letter* D?

"Look," Rhaina says quietly, taking Emma by the elbow and leading her away from the small crowd that has gathered. "You weren't born weird, okay? So take it from someone who was: it's not any fun. It's actually kind of awful. Don't do it. Try to blend in. Avoid being an outcast. Go back to being the popular girl you used to be."

Emma blinks at her. "Go back to the girl I used to be? Wow. Thanks for your input, but that's impossible. A lot of things would have to have *not happened.* I'd basically need to time-travel."

Rhaina says, low and urgent, "The people here—they can be vicious."

"I know," Emma says. "But they can say whatever they want about me. I don't care."

And it's astonishing to realize that she actually doesn't. When the flat well-wishes flooded into her text messages after her mother died, she felt cared for...until she actually responded honestly to the people who asked how she was doing.

She was supposed to say she was okay, she was supposed to act like she was okay, she was supposed to *be* okay. Anything else just meant emotional work for someone else, personal responsibility, and time spent away from furthering their own lives. Lives that would play out on a stage where the lights were dimming, and the actors were pretending not to notice.

"I don't care," Emma says again, relishing in the freedom of it.

"Well, I do," Rhaina says. "I care about you, even though I shouldn't, after how you treated me when—"

Emma is startled. "When what?"

But Rhaina only shakes her head, a clear veil of

disappointment shrouding her eyes. "You don't even remember."

"I don't," Emma admits. "But I am sorry. Actually, truly sorry."

Maybe Emma even likes Rhaina a little now, for being the one person brave enough to come up to her. But still.

"Just stop," Rhaina pleads.

"I can't," Emma says. "The things I'm talking about are way bigger than you or me. Way bigger than Ridgemont." She lifts her chin and yells, "*D* is for desertification, which is occurring thirty-five times faster than it used to!"

"You really don't see it, do you?" Rhaina says, stepping back from Emma. "You think you're going to make this big impact on the world, but all you're doing is dragging everyone around you down."

Emma stops, finally listening to someone else. "That's not true," she begins, but Mrs. Coleman, her French teacher, suddenly appears and says, "Ms. Blake, you're coming with me."

"Bonjour, madame," Emma says quickly. "Je préférerais ne pas aller avec vous—"

"I don't care if you'd rather not," says Mrs. Coleman through clenched teeth. "You *are*."

"Au revoir!" Emma calls to Rhaina, who's standing alone in the hallway now. "*F* is for fucked! As in we're all—"

CHAPTER 12

"EMMA BLAKE, I'M pleased to meet you," says Ridgemont Academy therapist Lori Bly, her voice warm and low.

"Are you now," Emma says dryly, gazing around the office, taking in everything from the black-and-white photos on the wall to the therapist's chic black suit and elegant silver bob. Emma thinks she'd wear her hair like that someday—no dye, no highlights—if she had any plans to get old. Which she doesn't.

"Can you talk to me about why you're here?"

"It was kind of a 'go-straight-to-the-shrink, do-not-pass-go' sort of thing," Emma says. She's sitting on a hard wicker chair, though Lori told her to make herself comfortable on the overstuffed couch. Her stomach grumbles. She missed breakfast, and now she's missing lunch. If she keeps going like this, she's going to starve before she burns.

"You're smiling," Lori says, producing one of her own.

Emma blinks. "Am I?"

"Faintly," the therapist clarifies, adjusting her smile to mirror Emma's.

"Weird. I don't know why." Emma digs her nails into the palms of her hands. The sharp tiny pain distracts her a little from the agony of her arm, and she's pretty sure it takes care of the smiling issue too.

Lori steeples her long fingers together underneath her chin. "I hear that you've been making some disturbing claims."

Emma decides to play a little dumb. "About climate change? They're not *claims*—they're true. And you should be disturbed. You should be terrified. Everyone should."

"I'm talking about burning yourself." Lori says this in an even tone.

Emma has to admit that there's no judgment in it. The woman is good at her job.

"Oh. That." God, what she'd give to fold her arms stubbornly across her chest! She should've burned the back of her hand, or something more out of the way.

"Do you want to talk about that?" Lori asks.

"Not really."

The therapist is quiet for what feels like five entire minutes. It's embarrassing, and Emma starts to squirm in her creaky chair. She's not sure if it's a trick to get her to fill the silence by suddenly opening up about her feelings, or if the idea of a student setting themselves on fire is just not all that interesting to the therapist.

"You must be hurting so badly," Lori finally says.

Emma deliberately misunderstands the statement. "Yeah. Burns suck. Don't get one if you can avoid it."

"That's not the hurt I'm talking about, and I think you know it."

Fine, she does. But it's not like she thinks this lady's going to be able to help. Back when she had friends, a few of them visited Lori, and they walked away gushing about how the woman had helped them get in touch with their feelings, access their inner self, and find a better path. Emma doesn't need any of that—she knows exactly how she feels, it's her outer self she's counting on to make her point, and the path she's walking has a termination point that is only getting closer.

"I remember when you came to Ridgemont as a ninth grader," Lori says. "You seemed so happy. You excelled in all your classes. You made JV soccer and the varsity tennis team, and you wrote an opinion column for the newspaper. You practically took the school by storm. But your *mother* had just died. And nobody would've known it! You never seemed to need any help at all."

Not *seeming* to need it is a lot different than not needing it, Emma considers pointing out. But she's guessing that's exactly what the therapist is getting at. Emma hides her feelings, Emma isn't in touch with her inner self.

"And you continued to excel," Lori goes on, "until recently."

Emma nods. "Sounds about right."

"Your sister's death changed everything, didn't it?"

Emma picks at her sleeve, aware that Lori isn't using the word, much like Hastings. She doesn't want to talk about this, doesn't want to think about how she was able to shoulder the loss of her mother because her sister was there for her, their shared grief making the weight seem less of a burden. The girls had been raised to succeed, and that meant getting out of bed, moving forward with life, and pretending like everything was going to be all right. They were strong, they were responsible, they were the Blake girls. But when Claire opted out of staying alive, being a Blake seemed so much harder.

"There are things that could make things a little easier for you," Lori finally says. "Medications, for example—"

"Kids at Ridgemont eat pharmaceuticals like M&Ms," Emma interrupts. "I'm not interested." She doesn't add her father's belief—that medication means admitting you can't handle life, that you crumble under the stress of just being a human.

Lori nods. "I hear your anger," she says.

Emma rolls her eyes. "Okay, whatever."

"Sometimes anger feels easier than sadness." She looks at Emma's arm. "And physical pain can feel better than emotional pain."

"Trust me," Emma says bitterly, "*none* of it feels good."

Lori reaches out and touches Emma's hand, just for an instant. "I'm listening."

Emma looks away when her eyes start filling with tears. It's a simple statement, but she can't remember the last time anyone actually told her they were listening to what she had to say.

Hastings shut down her article in the student newspaper.

Montgomery silenced her in the classroom.

Rhaina begged her to be normal in the hallway.

No one wants to hear what she has to say. Except maybe this person…someone whose job is to listen, someone who is being paid to listen.

Emma pulls her hand away from Lori and dashes away her tears, remembering something else her father told her. *Tears are like blood in the water for sharks. Spill a few, and a predator will move in.*

CHAPTER 13

EMMA CLEARS HER throat and fiddles with her mother's class ring, which she wears on her middle finger. "Fifty percent of my family is *dead,*" she says sharply. "I don't see how talking about it is going to make it any better."

Lori nods. "I'm not saying talking is magic. It doesn't bring anyone back to life. But keeping everything shut up tight inside you is dangerous."

Emma meets the therapist's calm gaze. *We don't even live in the same world,* she thinks. *You have no idea what it's like over here.*

But she says, "Fine. My mother died of cancer, and my sister killed herself. Happy now?"

"No, Emma, I would not say that I'm happy now. But I'm very sympathetic." Lori pushes her glasses up on her nose. "This isn't something I usually tell people, but I lost my brother to suicide."

Emma sits up straighter in her creaky chair. "How did he do it?" When Lori blinks at her response, Emma flushes and quickly adds, "I mean, I'm so sorry for your loss."

"Thank you," Lori says. She sighs. "He shot himself with our father's gun. He was eighteen years old." She gives an almost imperceptible shake of her head. "He would've been forty this year."

"I'm sorry," Emma says.

But she doesn't know if that's actually true. Lori is just trying to relate to her, show her that she understands her plight. But she so clearly does not. She thinks all of Emma's problems are rooted in the deaths of her family members, in her inability to reconcile her feelings. Emma would much rather talk about how her death will motivate others to facilitate change, to save the world. Lori hasn't asked *why* Emma wants to set herself on fire, which is the bigger question.

But no one has—not Montgomery, not Hastings, not Rhaina. They just want to know what is wrong *inside* her, not understanding that the world *outside* her matters so much more.

"What are you thinking now?" Lori asks, and Emma pulls her gaze away from the framed picture of a bird on the wall.

I want to see birds. Real birds.

Emma sighs. Maybe if she plays along she'll get out

of here faster. "I feel trapped," she says. "Trapped in this school, trapped in this office, and trapped inside my head." She digs her nails into her palms again, aware that a little bit of truth has slipped out. "Sometimes when I wake up in the middle of the night, it feels like I can't even breathe."

"What happens then?" Lori asks. "What do you do?"

"I lie there with this giant weight crushing me, and I just stay quiet until I can breathe again."

"Then can you fall back asleep?"

"I don't sleep much these days. But if you're going to suggest Ambien, don't."

I'll sleep when I'm dead was another of her father's sayings, repeated often as he hovered over his laptop, Mom telling him once again that he looked tired.

"Then I guess I'll look forward to cuddling with a corpse," Mom shot back once. But she beat him to that particular finish line.

"I wasn't going to suggest sleeping aids." Lori leans back in her chair and crosses one long leg over the other. "I want to hear about your sister, though, if you're willing. You must've been very close."

Emma certainly thought they were. But afterward, she realized how much Claire had been keeping from her. It makes her wonder if she ever knew her sister at all.

"She died in a car wreck on Christmas Eve." Emma's words come out flat and blunt. She can still hear her father's agonized voice on the other end of the line, the shock of hearing her father express something other than determination or anger making her legs collapse. Suddenly she was on the floor, and the ceiling was spinning above her. She has a scar on her chin from that fall. "It had snowed that morning, but she didn't hit a patch of ice. The police said there were no signs that Claire lost control of the car." She swallows the growing lump in her throat. "Or that she even tried to brake."

After a pause, Lori says, "That's so hard. I'm so sorry."

Emma knows it's what you're supposed to say—and she *just* said it to Lori—but she absolutely hates it when someone says it to her. ***You're*** *sorry?* she wants to scream. *Do you think that's going to make me feel better?* ***Nothing*** *can make me feel better. So you can take your "sorry" and shove it up your ass.*

"Can you tell me something else about her? About her life, I mean?"

Emma says, "Where am I supposed to start?"

Claire was everything to me.

"How about your first memory of her."

"Why?"

"You asked where you were supposed to start. The beginning seems like a good place."

Emma sighs. Fine. She'll play the game. She'll dust off the memory. Offer it up like a present no one really wants. Jump through the hoops Lori wants her to jump through.

"Okay. I was three years old. Claire had just turned

eleven, and for her birthday, my parents had this giant play structure built in our backyard," she says. "It had a tower, swings, slides, a climbing wall—everything. Claire was up in the tower with our neighbor, and I was supposed to be inside with the nanny. But I'd snuck out through the dog door, and I was standing underneath the tower, crying because I wanted to play with my sister. As soon as Claire heard me, she jumped out of the tower window and scooped me up in her arms. She put me in the baby swing and pushed me back and forth until I was screaming with laughter."

Emma grabs a tissue from Lori's coffee table. If she can't stop herself from crying, at least she can dry the tears before they fall. "It wasn't until later that night that anyone figured out she'd fractured her foot." Her eyes sting. "That was the kind of person Claire was. She took care of people. She looked out for me especially. I could always follow her lead." Emma wads up the tissue and flings it to the floor. "And now she's gone forever, and there's no one to tell me what to do or where to go or…I don't even know."

Lori hands Emma another tissue. "We don't want you to go anywhere," she says. "We want you to stay with us. We want to help you feel better. Do you think that might be possible?"

Emma runs her fingers through her short black hair. "I don't know that either," she says.

No fucking way, she thinks. *Because you still haven't asked me why.*

CHAPTER 14

KNOCK. KNOCK. KNOCK.

Emma lies motionless on her bed.

Knock knock.

"Emma?"

Emma turns her face toward the door but otherwise doesn't move.

"Emma, I know you're in there. Olivia told me. It's Jade."

"And Celia."

Knock.

Knock.

Emma watches as the doorknob turns and the door swings inward to reveal two girls who are still trying to be her friends. They're in their pajamas, with dewy, fresh-scrubbed faces. Celia is tall and stocky and blond.

Jade is tiny and thin and raven-haired. Celia stands nervously on the lavender shag rug that Olivia brought back after winter break—claiming that all the influencers had one now—but Jade just glides right in, smelling like skin cream and toothpaste.

"Hey you," she says in her charming accent. She's London born and raised, but her mother is an American Ridgemont alum. "God, this rug is minging, don't you think? It looks like unicorn vomit."

"I like it," Celia says, digging a toe into it. "It's soft."

She looks like she'd like to hide under it, Emma thinks. Like she'd rather look at unicorn vomit than at Emma's face. Which, given the length of time since Emma's bathed, might be understandable.

Jade flips her glossy black hair over her shoulder. "Celia's rank taste aside," she says, "we're sorry to barge in. You weren't asleep, were you?"

Sleep, what is sleep? "No," Emma says. "I was just, uh, resting."

Staring at the ceiling and checking the Doomsday Clock.

She tries to smile at them, but her face feels stiff and weird. She's touched they came to check in on her, but she wishes they hadn't bothered. They're going to do the same thing Lori did—ask her if she wants to talk, then press her into talking, then redirect the conversation to all the wrong things. If it were her birthday and she had a cake with seventeen candles on it, she'd blow them out and wish for everyone to leave her the hell alone.

"Can we sit?" Jade says, but she's already pulling out Emma's desk chair. Celia sinks into Olivia's.

"Make yourself at home," Emma says. Then she says what her mother used to say whenever one of her friends came to the house. "Can I offer you a snack?"

"What do you have?" Celia asks, but Jade shoots her a look, and Celia flushes pink. "Sorry, forget it."

Emma's mother, Sarah, used to keep homemade biscuits or banana bread on hand. There's no dorm oven, even if Emma knew how to bake, but at least Olivia knows how to buy snack food at Target. More than once, Emma has watched Olivia shoot a reel about how important a healthy diet is for good skin, only to open up a bag of Fritos afterward.

"Pringles," Emma says, pulling open Olivia's snack drawer. "Lärabars, gummy bears, ramen..."

"We'll pass, thanks," says Jade, tossing her hair to the other shoulder. Then she leans forward, puts her elbows on her knees, and says, "Emma, we just wanted to come see if you're okay." Her brow furrows prettily. "Not to be too blunt, but it sounds like you've been acting a bit nutters lately—"

"Jade," Celia squeals, flushing. "Have some *tact*."

"What I meant is that it sounds like things are hard for you right now, and I just want to say, we know what it's like to feel a little shit and alone—and we're here for you, okay? You're *not* alone."

Emma gives her a tiny nod. Of course she's not technically *alone;* she's got a roommate who says one thing and does the other; there are eight hundred students at Ridgemont, only 10 percent of whom she can't stand; and two of her friends are right here in the room. But ever since she came back after winter break—after Claire's funeral—there's been an invisible wall between Emma and everyone else. On one side of the wall is the normal world, with classes and friends and crushes and gossip. And on the other side is the grief world, where none of that matters at all. Emma lives there now. And *that's* where she's alone. In a place no one else can cross over to.

"Do you want to talk about it?" Celia asks.

Emma stiffens. "Do you remember when I tried to talk about it, but no one wanted to listen?"

Celia says, "Do you mean the thing you wanted to publish in the paper?"

"The *thing*?" Emma repeats bitterly.

Celia flushes again. "Sorry. I mean, the piece about your sister."

"Yes," Emma says. "That's exactly what I mean. Did you read it?"

"I never saw it. I just heard you arguing with Ms. Hofmann about it."

Emma reaches into her drawer and pulls out a coffee-stained page. “Here,” she says. “This is something I actually want to talk about, and what Ms. Hofmann didn’t want you to see.”

CHAPTER 15

In Memory of Claire: An Open Letter to Ridgemont Academy

My name is Emma Caroline Blake. But for as long as I can remember, I've had another name: Claire's Little Sister. I used to resent it. Now, though, I'd give anything to hear someone call me that.

Claire Isabelle Blake graduated from Ridgemont six years ago. Her list of achievements is too long to publish, so here are a few highlights: All-star tennis player. First chair violin. Senior class president. Valedictorian.

She went to Harvard, where she graduated

summa cum laude. Then she moved to New York City, where she became the youngest VP in her division at JP Morgan. She lived in a beautiful SoHo apartment with dozens of plants and one Siamese cat.

Claire Isabelle Blake had it all.

Did I mention that she was beautiful? That she knew a million jokes by heart? That she was the kindest, most generous person you'd ever meet?

Well, she was. But in the end, that didn't matter. None of it did.

This past December, while all of us were home for winter break, my sister, Claire, killed herself. She didn't leave a note, but I know why she did it.

She was miserable.

The dream child, the brilliant student, the perfect employee: Claire spent her entire life trying to live up to other people's expectations. Trying to be who they wanted her to be.

It broke her. And it started here at Ridgemont.

We have a reputation for academic excellence, and we're proud of that. We send so many kids to Harvard, they should pay us a finder's fee. But our never-ending pursuit of perfection has a dark side. A deadly side.

Relentless pressure leads to perpetual stress. And when anything less than perfection feels like failure, we all lose.

We're always being reminded of the opportunities our Ridgemont education offers—the life of wealth and success that awaits us. But what is the cost, besides $75,000 a year in tuition?

Our happiness? Our mental health?

Our *lives*?

Those of you who knew Claire knew what a magical person she was. Her smile was brilliant and her laughter was contagious.

She was the best of us.

But we asked too much of her.

Claire didn't deserve to die. And I didn't deserve to lose the person I loved most in the world.

Wake up, Ridgemont.

Sincerely,
Claire's Little Sister

CHAPTER 16

JADE COMES OVER and sits at the foot of Emma's bed. She circles Emma's ankle with her small, warm hand. "Love," she says. "That was beautiful. They should've let you publish it."

Emma shrugs. "Well, they didn't."

Celia seems to be at a loss for words. She's gazing down into her lap, her shoulders slumped.

"I'm glad you wrote it, even so," Jade says. "But you have to keep talking, Emma. You can't shut yourself away. You have to take care of yourself. And most importantly, you can't hurt yourself again. Claire wouldn't want that."

It doesn't matter what Claire wants anymore, does it? And why should I take care of myself when the world is ending?

Emma turns to the wall. She just wishes they would go

away. She isn't like them anymore, and there's no way she can make them understand this.

"I might want a Lärabar," Celia says softly, but no one acknowledges her. Emma wonders briefly if Lori might say Celia is eating her feelings.

"Claire was an amazing person," Jade says softly. "Remember how she'd come up from New York to take us out to pizza?"

Of course Emma remembers. The last time Claire took them to Vinnie's Pizza Pie was two months before she killed herself.

"We'd eat soooo much," Jade goes on, "and then she'd buy us a whole other pie to take back to the dorm."

"Vinnie's PP," Celia murmurs wistfully. "I haven't been there in ages."

"She always seemed so happy," Jade says. "So full of life and stuff."

"She was good at everything," Emma says, "including acting like she was happy. Acting the way everyone wanted her to—as if it was all okay and everything was going to turn out fine."

"You must miss her so much," Jade says.

Emma grits her teeth. *It must be so hard. You must miss her. You must be really struggling right now.* Why does everyone she ever talks to feel the need to state the totally fucking obvious? And why is no one listening? She just said she won't do what Claire did—pretend until she broke. She's done pretending. She'll be broken out in the open, and at least something she does will matter when she draws attention to a problem larger than Claire, larger than Ridgemont, larger than all of them.

"Have you thought about taking time off?" Celia asks. "Ridgemont's tough, like you said in your thing. I mean, your piece. Maybe you ought to give yourself a break."

Jade nods. "Would your dad let you?"

Everyone knows what a hard-ass Byron Blake is.

Emma rolls back over to face them. Of course he wouldn't. It isn't a question worth answering, just like all the others. "I'm fine," she says. "I'm just dealing with things in my own way."

Celia comes over to sit on the bed too, and the mattress sags with the weight of all three girls. "We miss you on the paper," she says.

Celia, Emma, and Jade were part of the *Ridgemont Trumpet* since the beginning. Jade was the gossip columnist and copyeditor; Celia was managing editor.

"Mr. Jordan promoted Soren to editor in chief, even though everyone knows he's a perfect *knob,*" Jade adds. "And I think Prue Bailey must be high, because her edits really suck lately."

Emma can't help smiling a little. "Her edits always sucked," she says.

"So you *don't* think she's taking hits off Caleb's bong before class. Interesting," Jade says. "Maybe we should investigate, Cel. Or we could run a blind item."

"Come back to the *Trumpet*," Celia blurts. "It can be like it was."

"No," Emma says, serious again. "It can't ever be like it was."

Jade lays her head down on Emma's long legs. "Babe," she says, "we love you. We miss you. We just want you to feel better."

"Look, I appreciate what you're doing," Emma says. "I know you're trying to help." Jade's silky hair spills over her shins. "But I'm fine. You guys need to worry about yourselves—there's the SATs coming up, plus the AP exams—"

"That reminds me, I'm *so* going to fail my French tomorrow," Jade mutters. "*Merde.*"

"Can you promise," Celia says, "that you'll talk to us if you need anything? And I mean *anything.*"

Emma realizes she does need something. "Can I borrow your car?"

Celia looks surprised for a second. Then she says, "Um, yeah, sure! Of course."

"Thanks a lot."

And Emma smiles genuinely, because now she's solved the problem of how to get a canister of gasoline.

CHAPTER 17

EMMA TOSSES AND turns in her dorm bed. Her burned arm throbs. Olivia's slow, steady breathing taunts her, reminding her of her own sleeplessness and the storm inside her that won't ever go quiet.

She rolls over, and her cozy blankets tangle in her legs. Her pillow wants to suffocate her. At night, all she can think about is everyone she's missing. All that she's lost.

It gets easier, everyone always says. *Sadness fades.*

These are the same damn people who say, *It must be so hard. You must miss Claire so much.*

They don't understand that *time equals loss.* It's a freaking law of nature. If Emma lets the years keep on passing, she's just going to keep on losing. So is everyone else, even if they can't bear to admit it. They just walk ignorantly through the world, turning away from anything they don't want to see.

But Emma sees all of it. And she needs them to know how bad things really are.

She decides that it's time to film another video. If anyone saw the first one, she hasn't heard about it. And what's the point of making a statement if no one knows you're making it? If she doesn't tell people about her plans, then she's just a tree falling in the forest, crashing down where no one can hear it land.

She isn't going to be the girl who burned but no one knew why.

She's going to make them understand.

Emma gets out of bed. Olivia gives a snort and rolls over, still sleeping peacefully. Emma grabs her phone and the ring light Olivia uses when she FaceTimes with her boyfriend at Choate. She slides open the closet door. Pushing aside the dresses that she stopped wearing after Claire died, she sits on the floor among the shoes. She turns on the light and flips her phone to selfie mode. She looks pale and ghostly, her black hair dissolving into the background dark. She looks like someone reporting from inside a grave. Or else somebody already dead.

Not that she cares. Vanity, like grades, doesn't matter when the world is on fire. When she'll be dead in a matter of days.

The closet is stuffy and smells like gym clothes.

She hesitates. It's a big deal to bare your soul. To make a promise like the one she's going to make.

But she has to be brave.

Emma reaches out and touches the red button.

"Hey," she says softly to the camera. "It's me again. Emma, remember? It's around two a.m., and I'm hiding in my closet. I wonder who's out there. I don't know if I'm talking to a hundred of you or only to my own face. I wish I could say that it didn't matter, but it does. I need you to hear me. To actually listen. And when I say *you*, I mean a lot of you."

She takes a deep breath. Brings her shoulders up tight to her ears and then lets them fall again. "It's weird how it feels easier to talk to a bunch of invisible strangers than it is to my friends. But I guess I feel like my friends don't really want to hear what I have to say. Or maybe they'd want to, but they wouldn't really be *able* to. It'd make them too uncomfortable. I've changed so much. But you—whoever you are—don't know what I used to be like. And you can believe what I'm telling you or you can think I'm crazy. You can listen super carefully or you can get bored and click over to a makeup tutorial or a Hype House video. I won't know. I'm not following the *metrics*. I'm not trying to be an *influencer*."

She stops for another breath. Tries to brush her bangs

away, but they fall back down, of course. She never should have cut them in the first place. "Or maybe I *am* trying to be an influencer. But I'm not trying to get you to buy skin products or whatever. I'm trying to get you to wake up and look around and understand what is going on. We're at the brink of total disaster. Everything is going wrong. And I literally mean *everything*."

She gives a light, false laugh. "*Oh, come on, Emma,* you're thinking, *don't exaggerate*. I'm not exaggerating. Little things, big things: *everything's* messed up. It's spring, right, with nice flowers and birds and all that? Well, the robins got here two weeks earlier than they're supposed to, because global warming changed their migration patterns. Robins will be okay for now. But what if I told you that three billion birds have disappeared from the skies in the last five decades? *Three billion!* That's more than the population of China and India put together." She hears a noise outside the closet and hits STOP. Olivia mumbles something in her sleep, gives a honking snore, and then goes quiet again.

"Speaking of which," Emma says, "we keep cramming more and more people onto the planet, and guess what—news flash, you guys—it *isn't getting any bigger*. Earth can't produce more fresh water, or more fertile soil, or more fossil fuels. We're using our natural resources up, and the more of us there are, the faster they're going to disappear. So why do we just keep drilling into the Arctic and driving our

SUVs and cutting down the Amazon and polluting our rivers like there won't be any consequences?"

She leans in closer and whispers. "By the way, people, do you know that you're full of *plastic*? We basically eat a credit card's worth of it every week. We don't notice, though, because they're microplastics, coming to us in our food and water. And from our leggings and our polar fleece. We're polluting the world *and* our own selves. We can see smog, or wildfire smoke, or beaches covered in trash, but we can't see the consequences of what we're doing to our bodies." She grimaces. "*Yet.* You're full of more weird chemicals than you can imagine, by the way, and we don't know what those do to us either. They call them forever chemicals because our bodies can't ever get rid of them."

Her voice begins to rise. Her anger's hot, like a flame. "What do you want to know about next? Modern-day slavery? Nuclear proliferation? Cyberwarfare?" She taps a finger at her temple. "Let's take door number one, that's fun. Did you know there are more than forty million people trapped in modern slavery? I'm talking forced marriage and forced labor. The palm oil in your lipstick, your toothpaste, and your Burger King got harvested by people forced to work for next to nothing. It also contributed to deforestation and destroyed orangutan habitat, if you care about that. And that T-shirt you're wearing? *Children* probably picked the cotton for it."

Emma gives a bitter laugh. "You're impressed with my handle on depressing facts, aren't you? I memorize this shit like the rest of my class memorizes Emily Dickinson for National Poetry Month. I don't want to do it. But I can't *not*."

She pushes her face right up to the camera. "When you know everything that I know, you can't just sit there pretending everything is okay. You can't even pretend that there's *hope* for the future. We've screwed up everything!"

Then she covers the camera lens so that only her voice is being recorded.

"The world is burning. But I'm going to burn first," she says. "Two days from now. Here, at Ridgemont Academy in the White Mountains of New Hampshire. And all of you can watch."

FIRE VIDEO # 2

Organdonor *2 hours ago*

mike grieve *5 hours ago*

wtff

Anniebananie *5 hours ago*

Omg this is so depressing

deadnaughtpirate *5 hours ago*

Someone call this girls parents

Narwhalmusic *5 hours ago*

"Im gonna burn 1st" this is fucken baller

Panda c *5 hours ago*

Do it do it do it

Misha *6 hours ago*

she srsly gonna do dis

GamerJo69 *6 hours ago*

i don't know u but i gotta say this is a bad idea

CHAPTER 18

Two days before the fire

EMMA'S VIDEO CATCHES fire. Pun…unavoidable.

Maybe it shouldn't surprise her the way it does. But Emma's only half awake, and she's barely thinking about anything at all as she walks into the dining hall for breakfast. As soon as she steps into the room, everyone goes dead quiet. Heads swivel in her direction. She hears someone whisper, "That's her, that's the girl. Emma Blake."

Emma whips around and walks right back out into the hall. Then she stands on the other side of the wall, breathing heavily. Heart going thump-thump-thump so hard her rib cage rattles.

Well, what did you expect? says one exasperated inner voice.

I didn't expect it quite this soon, says another.

Emma presses her palms flat against the cool tile. Feels the way the wall holds her up, even when her knees want to buckle. How long until someone comes and grabs her by the elbow and drags her off to the headmaster's office? Or the therapist's? Or maybe all the way to the psychiatric hospital in Concord?

It's a real problem when the thing you need to say is the exact thing that makes them want to shut you up.

Or lock you up, says voice number 1.

"Girl," Jade squeals, rushing out of the dining room and flinging herself at Emma. "What are you doing, do you understand what's happening?"

Emma says shakily, "I have a pretty good guess." Her arm begins to throb.

"The TikTok reaction video has already gotten almost a million views, and the West Coast isn't even awake yet."

Emma blinks at her. "The what?

Jade thrusts a phone into her face, though they're supposed to leave them in their rooms during the school day. "Look," she says, "you're going to freak out."

On the screen Emma watches a girl superimposed in front of her own YouTube video, nodding and pointing at text boxes—"Girl has a point," says one box; "wtf

BIRDS??!!??" says another—but she can't stand it anymore and turns away.

"I would think," she says quietly, "that what I had to say might be more interesting to you than some random's reaction video."

"It's not *random*. This is Kiara Chang. She has a jillion followers!"

"A jillion is not a real number. And you're still missing the point. You don't think I'm serious," Emma says. "You don't think I'm going to do it."

"Of course I don't think you're going to do it," Jade said, "because you're not totally fucking insane. You're just going through a hard time right now, and you're, like, acting out."

"And when did you get your degree in psychology?"

"Oh, Emma," Jade says, "don't be like that. You're not going to set yourself on fire. You're just not. You're not like that Buddhist bloke that Mr. Jackson told us about—"

"Thích Quảng Đức," Emma interjects, and yes, that is exactly who she is like. Or…wants to be.

"Yeah, him, you're not going to burn in the middle of a street somewhere!"

That's right, I'm going to do it here on campus.

"I love you," Jade says pleadingly, but her eyes are still on her phone, watching as some influencer's reaction to Emma's video gets more views than the original. "You know I do."

"Love you too," Emma says hollowly.

"Walk with me to first period. Talk to *me*, darling, not to strangers on the Internet. I care about the earth too. I care about all of it! But mostly I care about you. I don't want to see you acting like this."

Emma shakes her head. She can't deal with Jade right now; she can't deal with anyone. "I have to run back to my room. I forgot my graphing calculator. You know how mad Brighouse gets when we're not prepared."

"Oh," Jade says, her face falling a little. "Okay. Well, I'll see you at lunch, right?"

"Right," Emma says, and she hurries away before Jade can say anything else.

She cuts across the grass, which students aren't supposed to do, because she doesn't want to meet anyone on the paths. She passes under a magnolia tree, and the white blossoms fill the air with sweetness.

A thought stops her in her tracks—*I'll miss this smell*—but she quickly hurries on. The magnolia might be dead in a few years due to climate change. If she stops to smell the metaphorical roses now, they won't be here in the future.

Emma opens the door to her dorm and goes down the hall to her room. The walls are painted an ugly yellow and hung with Olivia's dumb Broadway musical posters, but the sunlight streams through the big window and warms her bed and makes the white duvet glow.

She falls face down on her pillow, with its pale rose velvet case. She doesn't want to get up. It doesn't matter that she doesn't know where her graphing calculator is. She's failing math. So what. What does math matter when she posted about three billion birds dying—an actual scientific fact—but all Jade cares about is some influencer's *jillions* of followers?

She hears voices in the hallway. There's a trill of laughter. Someone with a southern accent is talking about a spring dance. Someone else is regretting a sext that she sent to her ex-girlfriend.

None of it matters.

They don't understand this, but Emma does.

"She showed it to everyone on the field hockey team!" the voice cries.

Who cares, who cares, who cares, Emma whispers into her pillow, and she keeps on saying it until the cops come crashing through her door.

CHAPTER 19

EMMA BOLTS UP, gives a shriek of fear, and clutches her pillow to her chest like it's a bulletproof shield.

"Are you all right?" says the first one urgently, a woman with a long blond braid pulled over one shoulder. Her name tag identifies her as D. Wozniak.

The other one, a man, says, "Emma Blake?" Emma doesn't bother getting his name. A quick glance tells her this is campus police, not the real cops. Law enforcement JV team has been sent in.

"We're here for a safety check," Wozniak says. "Don't be alarmed."

"Oh, I'm not alarmed." Emma throws the pillow aside. "I just might have pissed myself. What are you doing here?"

"We received a call that you were in danger," Wozniak says.

"I was lying down! The only danger was you people *scaring* me to death! You could've knocked!"

Wozniak nods, but the man says, "We had reports of a threat—a threat of self-harm. Given the situation, we felt it would be prudent to enter."

Never admit anything, her father likes to say, *even when the other side has proof.*

"Kicking someone's door down is hardly prudent," Emma says. "Like I said, I was just resting. I have a headache. And thanks to you, I nearly had a heart attack."

Her heart's still pounding, her thoughts racing. Outwardly, she'll be casual with the rental police, but inside, she's freaking out. Who made the call? Who narced?

Jade, it better not've been you.

"We'd like to take a look around your room if that's all right," Wozniak says, but the male officer is already pulling out drawers, not waiting for an answer.

"Why? What are you looking for?" Emma asks.

They glance at each other. Emma glares at each one of them in turn.

"Do you think I have a *weapon* or something? I don't have any weapons! Why don't you look for my graphing calculator? I haven't been able to find it for days."

"We don't actually need your permission," Wozniak says.

"Oh, so you're just being polite?" Emma doesn't even try to keep the sarcasm out of her voice. "Gee, thanks."

"Emma, Emma, what on earth is going on in here?" Mrs. Vickers pushes her way past the campus police and stops in front of Emma's bed. She's still wearing her fuzzy slippers, and her hair is in old-fashioned rollers.

"Ask *them,*" Emma says. "All I know is that I came back to the dorm because I forgot something, and the next thing I know there's a SWAT team in my room. A severely underfunded SWAT team," she amends, hoping to get a crack in.

Mrs. Vickers turns to the officers, and her tone sharpens. "Emma is a lovely, mature, and trustworthy girl. You can't just barge in on her like this! If you knew what she's been through..."

Mrs. Vickers is suddenly Emma's favorite person in the world.

"Ma'am," Wozniak begins, "it's because of what Emma has been through that we were instructed—"

"She's been under a lot of strain lately, poor thing," the dorm monitor goes on, "and having you two bursting into her room is hardly going to help with that!" Her voice rises in pitch as she works herself into a maternal fury.

"Ma'am," the male officer says, "we're here because we were called by a concerned member of the Ridgemont community."

"And as another concerned member of the Ridgemont community, I am going to ask you to leave." Mrs. Vickers even shakes a skinny finger in his face. "I'll take care of her. I'm her dorm mother, and that's what she needs right now. A mother. Not a shakedown!"

"But ma'am—"

"The proper term is *madame,*" Mrs. Vickers says stiffly. "I am of French extraction."

French extraction? This is news to Emma. "*Merci,*" she whispers. "*Je t'aime,* Madame Vickers. *Je t'aime* so much."

Meanwhile, the male officer is eyeing the one drawer he opened, fingers twitching to dig in.

"I swear to God, creeper," Emma says, "if you touch my underwear—"

Wozniak, looking uncomfortable now, fiddles with her braid. "Look—" she starts to say, but then Headmaster Hastings barges into the room. His tie's slanted, and his pocket square's about to fall out. He's out of breath.

"Mr. Hastings," Mrs. Vickers says, "tell these people—"

"The police are here for Emma's protection, Mrs. Vickers," he says firmly. He squares his shoulders. "They will be searching her room for weapons."

"Weapons?" Emma repeats, incredulous. "I'm not a school shooter. I don't have anything dangerous in here. As I already told these two."

I haven't bought the gas yet.

"Emma," Mr. Hastings says sternly. "You know very well that we're not worried about you being a harm to others."

He nods to the male officer, who practically dives at Emma's dresser, thick fingers pawing through her things.

Emma puts her head in her hands. She wasn't expecting this. She just wants it to be over. "It was a joke," she says. Her voice is muffled. Then she looks up, pleading. "A prank. I didn't really mean it."

A variety of expressions cross Mr. Hastings's face. Anger. Disbelief. Hope. "A prank," he says quietly. Then he sighs. "I wish I knew that I could believe you."

Emma blinks innocently as Wozniak picks up a pair of scissors and deposits them into a ziplock bag. Emma's letter opener—a present from her grandma that she's never once used—slides into the bag beside it.

"Do they really need to take my school supplies?" Emma asks Mr. Hastings.

"They will be taking any sharp objects. And I will be calling your father. Again."

He looks so unhappy about this that Emma nearly laughs. She gets it: she wouldn't really want to talk to her father right now either. "Ask him about Marcus Aurelius," she says.

"What? Why?"

Emma shrugs. "My dad quotes him a lot."

"I fail to see what that has to do with you," he says stiffly. A bead of sweat slips down his cheek.

Poor Mr. Hastings. Who's he supposed to believe, the

kid who says she's going to burn herself alive or the father who insists she won't? Between the two of them, Mr. Hastings is in way over his head. Worse still, he looks like he might already know it.

"Nothing," Emma says. "But he might be nicer to you that way."

CHAPTER 20

AS THE COPS are pawing through the closet, and Emma and Mr. Hastings are staring at each other, an unfamiliar young woman with short chestnut hair slithers into the room. "Emma Blake?"

Who the hell is this?

Hastings must recognize the new arrival, because a look of barely repressed fury fills his face. He tries to block her from advancing any farther into the room. "We don't need you here. You are on private property—"

"Good morning, Mr. Hastings," the woman says brightly. "Nice to see you too."

She darts past the headmaster and over to where Emma is sitting on the bed. Mrs. Vickers has to scramble out of her way.

"Emma, my name is Rachel Daley, and I'm a reporter with the *Boston Globe*." She hooks a thumb in the headmaster's direction. "I used to be with the *Union Leader* here in New Hampshire, which is how Mr. Hastings and I became friends."

She says the word *friends* with a touch of sarcasm, drawing out the *s* at the end so it comes out as a menacing hiss.

Meanwhile Hastings is audibly grinding his teeth. "This is private property, Ms. Daley," he says. "I can't imagine how you heard about Emma's situation, but I'm afraid you'll have to go."

"How I found out?" Rachel asks, real confusion clouding her eyes. She glances at Emma, who shakes her head. If Hastings doesn't know about the YouTube video yet, Emma certainly doesn't need him finding out now. He'll probably have the cops take all of her shoelaces too.

"Emma is in perfectly good hands, and you need to leave," Hastings says, pointing out the door. "If I have to ask the officers to escort you out, I certainly will. This is a Ridgemont issue, concerning only Ridgemont staff and students. There's no reason for the public—"

"Does the entire Internet count as public?" Rachel whispers into Emma's ear. Emma doesn't know if this woman has her back or is threatening to tell Hastings about the YouTube video, but either way, she needs to keep her here… and keep her happy.

"Why should she leave?" Emma asks. "It's already a freaking party in here, so what's one more?"

"Mr. Hastings doesn't like me," Rachel says to Emma. "I wrote a piece about private schools—you know, their elitism, their inequity, the way they brush any harmful or shady occurrences under the rug—that he found objectionable." She turns to smile glitteringly at Hastings. "But it's all water under the bridge, as far as I'm concerned." She sits down on the end of Emma's bed. "Why I'm here today has nothing to do with Ridgemont," she says, "and everything to do with you. I saw your video. You're putting out a powerful message, Emma Blake."

She gives Emma's leg an affectionate little tap.

Emma scoots away—*I don't know you, don't touch me*—but she's thrilled that her message has gotten to someone who's paying attention, while also being not thrilled at all that this stranger just outed her in front of Hastings. She didn't make the video so Kiara Chang could hijack her content or random TikTokers could set her words to music. The whole point was to be taken seriously. *The world is in grave danger.*

"Video?" she hears Mr. Hastings saying. "What video?"

And that pretty much *guarantees* she's going to be taken seriously now. The only problem is, Rachel might have also just made it impossible for Emma to carry her plan out.

Rachel withdraws her hand from Emma's leg. "Sorry," she says. "I have four younger sisters—we're touchy!"

Claire and Emma weren't touchy. They were *talky*.

Whether Claire was at Ridgemont, Harvard, or JP Morgan, she would call Emma every Sunday at 3:00 p.m. on the dot. "How's my little sis?" she'd ask, and Emma would say, "Little? I'm taller than you are," and Claire would pretend like this was news. "Really, when did that happen?" And Emma would laugh and say, "When I was in seventh grade!" The whole silly routine was just how they said *Hello, it's me, I miss you.*

They texted and called and wrote actual letters, with nice stamps and beautiful stationery. They told each other everything.

Or so Emma thought.

Oh Claire, oh Claire, why didn't you tell me how much you were hurting?

Wozniak knocks over a pile of shoeboxes with a clatter. "Sorry!"

Jones is still pawing through Emma's drawer. He pulls out a long, narrow velvet box.

"It's a fountain pen," Emma tells him. "Not a weapon."

Jones opens the box, stares at the contents, and tucks it into the bag anyway.

"Do you think it's right for them to be doing this to you?" Rachel asks Emma.

"Doesn't seem like I can stop them," Emma says, watching as all of her socks end up on the floor next to her underwear.

"Do they have reasonable suspicion that they'll turn up something illegal?" Rachel asks, glaring at Hastings.

"It's time for you to leave, Ms. Daley," Hastings says.

"But she's my guest. I—I invited her," Emma says quickly. Anything to keep a reporter in the room long enough to slow Hastings down and buy Emma some time to figure out what she's going to do.

Rachel doesn't miss a beat. "Yes, Emma reached out to me directly," she says.

"Is this true?" Hastings asks.

"Yes," Emma says. Her lie has more to do with having a tiny bit of control over this dorm room chaos than it does with keeping Rachel Daley around, but whatever. "I'm not some damaged person who's got to be protected from herself." She thrusts out her wrists. "Look! Not so much as a scratch!"

"What about the third-degree burn?" Hastings asks.

"This isn't some suicidal fantasy I'm having!" Emma cries, ignoring the question. "Don't you see this isn't about me?"

"What is it about, then?" Hastings asks quietly.

"It's about the entire world," Emma says. Suddenly she can feel tears stinging in the corners of her eyes. "And how completely, totally *fucked* it is."

"Language, Emma!" Mrs. Vickers gasps.

"Sorry," Emma says. "I mean, *le monde est foutu*."

The baffled look on Mrs. Vickers's face is proof that while she may be of French extraction, she does not actually speak French. But it doesn't matter.

And maybe it doesn't even matter that two rent-a-cops are snooping through her stuff, or that Hastings is about to call her dad, or that she's never going to find her graphing calculator.

In just a few days, she'll be gone forever.

CHAPTER 21

HASTINGS SINKS INTO his office chair and drums his fingers on the desk as Fiona calls Byron Blake for the third time in three days. Hastings is sweaty and anxious and furious at everyone.

At the beginning of Emma's downward spiral, he hoped that this was an expected footnote to her grief, a bump in the road for a girl who had always been flying along in a Mercedes-Benz, and that she would likely recover quickly. As things escalated, some part of him—he realizes now—wondered if Emma was acting out, creating a scene as an emotional outlet. But the hollow look in her eyes as she watched campus security toss her room has led Hastings to consider the unthinkable: Emma is serious. And now he has to convince her father of that.

Fiona signals thumbs-up, and Hastings picks up his phone.

"Hold for Mr. Blake," says that same smooth British voice, and a split second later the man himself is seething into the headmaster's ear.

"What is it *now*?"

Mr. Hastings clears his throat. "Sir, I wouldn't keep calling if I weren't deeply concerned about your daughter." *Believe me,* he adds silently, *I hate talking to you.* "There have been…developments since yesterday—"

Blake cuts him off. "You didn't let her hurt herself again, did you?"

"*Let?*" Mr. Hastings repeats, incredulous.

He takes a deep breath, reminds himself of the money Blake donates every year, and tries to keep his tone even. "No one allowed your daughter to harm herself yesterday," he says. "I'm not even sure anyone could have stopped her in regard to the Bunsen burner." *Except herself,* he adds silently. *Which is why I'm calling. Please, hear me.*

"Today I'm calling because she has made another disturbing and specific threat about self-immolation. And she did it in a video that she posted to YouTube. We think that—"

"YouTube?" For the first time, something cracks in Blake's voice, even if it is only concern for the reputation of his family name. "Make her take it down immediately!"

"I *have*," Mr. Hastings says. He doesn't mention that others have reposted the video—that once something's online, it's almost impossible to take it off again—or that Emma herself could put it back up any minute. He learned long ago that policing the Internet is a never-ending task.

"But I believe we need to take her threats seriously." He takes a deep breath. Works up the nerve to say what he needs to say next. "Mr. Blake, one of the greatest risks for suicide is *exposure* to suicide. When Emma's sister killed herself, she put Emma at a much greater risk of doing the same thing." His heart pounds as he waits for Blake's reply.

"Emma," the man says after several moments, "is not her sister." His voice is thick, like it's hard for him to say the words. "Claire was in therapy ever since she was twelve. She was hospitalized twice when she was at Ridgemont. But she was still the valedictorian, did you know that? No, you wouldn't; it was before your time. Her second semester at Harvard, she ended up at McLean in a locked ward. But she got herself out, and she graduated at the top of her class. She was incredible. Brilliant and driven and successful."

"I've heard," Hastings says quietly. "I'm so sorry."

It's not clear that Blake hears him. "But Claire was not stable, and she was not happy."

Hastings hazards a sentence. "Emma doesn't seem very happy either."

"Of course not!" Blake yells. "Her mother and sister

are dead! She's a young girl and she's grieving." There's a moment of near silence, when all Hastings can hear is Blake's controlled breathing.

"But she is strong," Blake finally continues. "Unlike Claire, she's stable. And she is not going to set herself on fire."

"With all due respect—"

"With all due *respect,*" Blake interrupts, "I know my daughter much better than you do. If I believed Emma was actually in danger, I'd be there by lunchtime. Emma is only testing boundaries. She's dealing with her grief in her own way, and you need to let her do that."

Hastings mimes smashing the phone into the polished surface of his desk. "Mr. Blake, we cannot have students proclaiming their intention to burn themselves to death! Emma needs to take a break from school and—"

"Emma is just like me, Hastings. Work is what makes her happy. Work is what makes her keep going. Having a purpose, fulfilling a function—that's why we're here, all of us. Maybe the real problem is that *you're* not fulfilling your function. Maybe Ridgemont isn't giving Emma enough purpose. Maybe it's all too easy for her and she's bored, so she's finding ways to keep herself busy."

Hastings bristles. "Ridgemont remains one of the top schools in the state, sir, and we are handling this situation as best we can. However, it seems clear that Emma needs more support than we can provide for her here."

Sweat drips down his nose as stress raises his body temperature. He pulls his tie loose, opening his collar, a heat wave passing over him. He tries not to think about Emma's essay, her description of fire consuming human flesh. "We want to ensure that she's safe, and that she gets the help she needs. We can arrange for her to receive all her class assignments while she's focusing on—"

"Are you threatening to suspend my daughter?" Blake's voice has gone icy. "Because that's what it sounds like. But I'm sure you wouldn't be so stupid. For the last time, my daughter is fine. I know what she's doing. *She* knows what she's doing. Don't ruin her life by acting like this is something it isn't."

Hastings thinks about all those Marcus Aurelius quotes he's read, just in case they might help him with Blake. One in particular springs to mind: *Everything we hear is an opinion, not a fact. Everything we see is a perspective, not the truth.*

Blake thinks his perspective *is* truth.

"Mr. Blake," Hastings begins. "My intent is not to ruin Emma's life. I'm trying to save it. If you would consider—" But Blake doesn't let him get one syllable further.

"Be very careful about any action you're thinking about taking. It's one kind of pain to lose a donor. But lawsuits, Mr. Hastings, are a different thing altogether. They are very expensive. And they are *very* bad publicity."

Hastings swallows with difficulty. The last thing he wants is a lawsuit.

Actually—take that back.

The last thing he wants is for Emma Blake to die in a wave of flames.

"Sir," he says, "don't think of it as a suspension. Think of it as a leave of absence. We may need to insist—"

But Byron Blake has hung up.

CHAPTER 22

WITH BLAKE'S THREAT still ringing in his ears, Hastings dials the law offices of Forbes, Miller, and Rumswell. George Forbes—Ridgemont class of '89, Yale Law '95—picks up directly and says, "I've been meaning to call. Can we push the match to ten?"

"I'm not calling about tennis, George," Hastings says. "We have a situation."

"You know how I feel about that word," George says cheerfully.

Actually, Hastings doesn't know. Is George happy for the potential business or concerned about his alma mater? He doesn't ask. And George quickly sounds less cheerful as the headmaster fills him in on Emma Blake's threats and the conversation with Byron Blake.

Thankfully George is better at situations than he is at returning a flat serve. Calmly he lays out the plan for Emma Blake's immediate future at Ridgemont.

"Emma Blake should probably be admitted to a psychiatric hospital," George says. "But she doesn't want to go, and her father doesn't want her to go, and I doubt you could have her committed. You could take her to the ER and file an Involuntary Emergency Admission petition, but it sounds like she'd present to any attending doc as fully in her right mind."

"Yes," Hastings says grimly. "She's very well spoken and reasonable, unfortunately. That's about the long and short of it. So what do you recommend?"

"We have to ensure Emma's safety above all else," George goes on. "She needs careful supervision. Is there somewhere she can stay that's not her dorm? A place that can be monitored more closely?"

Hastings thinks for a moment. "There's a room we sometimes use for visiting lecturers. It's right near the counselor's office, and we could have someone outside all night if we needed to."

"You need to," George says decisively. "Make sure she's comfortable and looked after. And document everything, Perry. Every precaution you take. Every call you make. You need to do everything you can to ensure Emma's safety—but you have to ensure your own too."

CHAPTER 23

RACHEL DALEY PEERS at the gilt-framed pictures Emma keeps on her bookshelf. She gets so close to them that her freckled nose nearly touches the glass. When she turns around, she smiles and says, "You're such a beautiful family."

"*Were* such," Emma says.

What seems like a flicker of confusion crosses Rachel's pale, fine-boned face. "What?"

"The verb's past tense," Emma says. She kicks off her shoes. Crosses her legs underneath her. The cops are gone, and she's not going to math class today. She's probably never going to math class again. But she doesn't want to talk to Rachel Daley about her dead family members. "Never mind."

Rachel gestures to the end of Emma's bed. "Can I sit?"

It's weird that she's asking now, when earlier she just flopped down and started patting Emma's leg, but Emma shrugs. "Make yourself at home." She doesn't offer Rachel a snack. Last time she did that, someone narced on her. Hospitality apparently doesn't pay.

Rachel pulls out her phone. "I was hoping we could talk more openly."

Emma eyes the iPhone. It's an old model, and the screen is beat to hell. "And you want to record me?"

"If you agree."

Emma shakes her head. "I don't feel comfortable."

"But you've already put out two videos—"

"I made those. I was in control of them," Emma says. "How do I know you won't twist my words? Won't make me sound crazy? I know how easy it is to splice together something that changes my meaning, even if my words are the same."

"I would never."

Maybe, maybe not. The truth is that Emma doesn't know Rachel Daley, and trust doesn't exactly come easily to her. "I don't understand why you want to write about me anyway. What brought you here all the way from Boston?"

"When a girl says that she's going to set herself on fire to protest the state of the world, that's news," Rachel says. "I want to tell that story. *Your* story."

"The videos said it all," Emma says stiffly. "I already told it."

Rachel nods. "A lot of people saw them, before you had to take them down."

"So I've heard."

Rachel scoots closer to her. "What do you think is the worst problem humanity's facing?"

Emma snorts. "Gee, how do I pick? Climate change is going to kill most of humanity eventually. But a nuclear bomb from a rogue state could start a war that kills everyone in a matter of days."

"You don't sound like you have a lot of hope."

"That's because I don't." Emma's hope died with Claire. Maybe that's when her trust went too.

Rachel lifts a shoulder in a half shrug. "You're young. Brilliant. Rich. You have a lot of power, Emma. You could be a voice for change."

"I *am* a voice for change," Emma says. "People are going to listen to me. They're going to listen to me because they're learning from my videos. Think about it: if what I'm saying isn't true, I sure as shit wouldn't burn for it."

Every time Emma says it, it becomes more real.

When exposed to heat, the muscles in my thighs will shrink and retract along the shafts of my femur...

Rachel is quiet for a minute. She fiddles with her phone, rubbing her thumb across the cracked glass, her brow furrowed. Emma watches the reporter out of the corner of her eye. Once, she thought she might be like Rachel: young, ambitious, hungrily seeking out stories that mattered to people. Emma loved running the Ridgemont newspaper, kept notebooks full of story ideas.

Last fall she was planning a summer internship at the *New York Times*. But then Claire died, and everything fell apart, and now the only thing Emma is planning is her own death.

Rachel looks up, and her cool gray eyes search Emma's face. "I have to ask," she says. "Is some of your despair about the state of the world motivated by your own personal tragedies?"

Emma sits upright, startled. She clutches the pillow to her chest again.

"Yes, I know about your sister," Rachel says softly. "And your mom. I never talk to anyone without googling them first. It's the first law of reporting. Dating, too, for that matter. And Emma—I can't imagine what it must be like to lose two people so close to you. I'm so sorry."

"Yeah, me too," Emma snaps. "It really fucking sucks." She digs her nails into the pillow. "But if you just found out about it on Google, I don't think you really care. So don't ask me if I want to talk about it."

"I won't," Rachel says. "But would you be willing to talk more about your fears for the world? You know so much about the issues we're facing."

"No," Emma stands up. "Thanks for asking. I'm glad you're not trying to bury your head in the sand like everyone else. I'm glad you see that we're killing ourselves and all the other species on this planet. But this is my story to tell, and I'm going to tell it on my own terms."

CHAPTER 24

To: lbly@ridgemontacademy.edu

Subject: Emma Blake

Lori: Per our last convo, please prep Rose Room for Emma's overnight stay. Have housekeeping remove computer and TV. We want her to focus on rest.

She should be in before 7 p.m. and monitored at all times.

PH

To: phastings@ridgemontacademy.edu

Subject: re: Emma Blake

Yes but I don't think isolating her from the student population is wise. Can we get her some visitors? I can reach out to folks.

To: lbly@ridgemontacademy.edu

Subject: re: re: Emma Blake

Lori: Yes, good idea. We will have a guard too. For her safety.

PH

To: phastings@ridgemontacademy.edu

Subject: re: re: re: Emma Blake

Let me do it. She trusts me. As much as she seems to trust anyone, anyway.

To: lbly@ridgemontacademy.edu

Subject: re: re: re: re: Emma Blake

Lori: Thank you. It is of the utmost priority that we keep Emma Blake safe.

CHAPTER 25

"WAIT A SECOND. You want me to sleep here?" Emma asks, incredulous. Lori Bly, the therapist, and the school nurse have just tag-teamed her outside the dining hall and led her, protesting, straight to Pemberly Hall.

Lori lightly touches Emma's shoulder. Emma flinches like she's been burned. "Just for a night or two," she says. "So you can rest."

Emma takes a reluctant step into the room. It's on the second floor, with two large windows looking out onto the quad. On the left is a queen-size bed with a pink comforter and six decorative pillows. Two polished bedside tables sport matching brass lamps and fake succulents. There's a desk, an overstuffed armchair, and an antique trunk with a vase of real pink roses on top. Everything is clean, impersonal; the air smells like furniture polish.

"The poet Mark Plante stayed here last year when he came to lecture—did you see him?" Lori smiles. "Quite a few illustrious people have slept in this room, in fact."

"But illustriousness is not why *I'm* here," Emma says. She knows what this is: a pretty jail cell. A gilded cage. "I don't have any of my things. What about my toothbrush and pajamas? My laptop? My homework?"

Never mind that she's been blowing off homework all semester. Never mind that she's usually too wrecked to brush her teeth at night, or that she barely sleeps in the first place. Never mind that she only uses her laptop for posting incendiary YouTube videos. Grades, gingivitis, insomnia—they don't matter when you're dead.

Lori's voice is gentle when she answers. "I know this isn't what you want, Emma. But it's important for you to be here. A lot of people are worried about you. We need to keep you safe."

Emma walks over to the casement window, cranks it open, and leans out. Twenty feet below: hydrangea bushes, not yet blooming, and the footpath to the library and the theater building. "It wouldn't be hard to jump," she says mildly. "If I really wanted to get out of here."

Why does she even say this? She's not going to jump. It's not part of the plan, and it certainly wouldn't kill her. Also, she knows enough about her rights to know that they can't keep her here against her will.

In an instant, Lori's hands are on Emma's shoulders again, and this time her touch isn't gentle. "I need you to promise me that you're not going to do that." The therapist's gaze is frightened. Urgent.

"I'm not going to jump out the window," Emma says. She's really not, so it's an easy promise to make. She pulls away from the therapist's grip. "I'm also not going to hurt myself in my dorm room, so I think you should let me go back there."

I could burn in the newspaper office. Or at the Ridgemont radio station. Somewhere in the media arts building, anyway. I need a door with a lock.

Am I going to have to disable sprinklers? I don't know how to disable sprinklers.

"Like I said," Lori says, "this is only temporary. I'll have Jade pack up your things. What do you need to make yourself comfortable here?"

Emma realizes that there's no talking her way out of this, at least not tonight. She sighs. She perches on the ledge of the open window, purposely trying to make Lori nervous, as she reluctantly lists the items she wants—her velvet pillow, her slippers, her sweatpants, Advil. When she mentions her laptop and phone, though, Lori shakes her head.

"Tonight should be a time of pure rest," she says.

Emma widens her eyes at her. "You're afraid I'm going to make another video!"

Lori chooses to ignore this, which means that Emma's right.

"You can read a book, write in a journal...There's a radio here, see?" Lori smiles. "You can just enjoy a little peace and quiet."

"I haven't been able to enjoy anything since Claire died," Emma snaps. "Don't make this out like it's some kind of staycation. This is Ridgemont's version of a padded cell."

"Emma"—Lori sighs—"we aren't locking you up. We're just keeping an eye on you."

"Is there a cot? Are you going to sleep here too? Should we make it a goddamn slumber party?" With each sentence, Emma's volume climbs. This isn't how the plan was supposed to go. She was going to borrow Celia's car tonight, but now she's locked in the administration building.

"Someone will be outside your door, but you will have privacy, don't worry," Lori says gently. "But I think there are some people who'd like to come see you."

Emma rolls her eyes. "Great. Visiting hours at the jail."

She walks over to the window again, her thoughts like dark clouds, swirling. She wonders if she could get Pringles and a canister of gas from Circle K with Uber Eats.

"Can I get you anything?" Lori asks. "Tell me what you need."

A gallon or two of unleaded, Emma thinks.

"No," she says.

CHAPTER 26

THE PEMBERLY GUEST room is twice as big as Emma's dorm double, and it takes her twelve seconds to make a lap. She feels like a cheetah in a zoo, wearing a path around the perimeter of a chain-link enclosure.

Cheetahs are threatened with extinction due to habitat loss, poaching, and the illegal pet trade.

She makes her hands into fists. *Come on, Emma. Figure it out, problem solver. How do you overcome the obstacles and achieve the goal?*

Three species of tigers are already extinct.

She pauses at the window. It's evening now, and the light slants golden across the quad. She can see Elliott passing a football with a senior whose name she forgets. Braydon or Caden or Aiden—another rich white boy with a beach house on Cape Cod and a spot waiting for him at Harvard in the fall.

You think the world can't touch you, she thinks, as he runs toward the ball with an easy, graceful lope.

She almost feels sorry for him, this boy who has everything. Someday he'll realize how messed up the world is. Maybe it will be when the economy crashes and he can't get that six-figure job that was supposed to land in his lap. Maybe it will be when he finds out there's not enough water in the world for everyone and he googles how a person dies from dehydration. Maybe it will be when his first child is born with a serious congenital issue because the mother's body is loaded with microplastics. But whatever it is, and however long it takes, when it does happen, it's really going to suck for him. Because it'll be the first time he loses something.

Emma knows this firsthand. That's because she had everything once too.

The senior catches the ball one-handed. Does a goofy end-zone dance.

"Wake up," Emma whispers to him. "Wake up and smell the dumpster fire of your future."

A knock sounds on the door, and Emma steps away from the window. "Yeah?"

"Can I come in? It's Ms. Reddington." The teacher gives a small, nervous-sounding laugh. "I mean, *may* I."

Ms. Reddington was Emma's ninth-grade English teacher. She introduced Emma to Jane Austen and Evelyn Waugh, *Jude the Obscure* and *Madame Bovary.* She marked up Emma's essays in red pen and told her she had talent; she encouraged her to start writing for the *Trumpet*.

Emma hesitates, then says, "Sure, okay." Maybe it'll be nice to talk to her old teacher again. Even if it's awkward, it'll probably be more fun than pacing the generically pretty room like a caged animal.

The door swings inward, and Ms. Reddington is there in a yellow dress, her big brown eyes full of concern. "Hi, Emma," she says. "It's been a minute, hasn't it? I just wanted to check in—you know, see how you're doing."

"I've been better."

"Oh, honey," Ms. Reddington says sympathetically. She looks like she wants to give Emma a hug, but Emma takes an almost imperceptible step backward. Rachel Daley wore out her human touch meter for the day, thank you.

"Have a seat," Emma says. Suddenly she's nervous. She can feel her pulse quickening, and words come tumbling out of her mouth. "I wish I could offer you something, but I've got nothing here. In the dorm we have snacks, and I have a mini fridge. I keep all kinds of different seltzer flavors in it, and Olivia uses it to keep her face masks cold. She's a skin-care obsessive. Basically a walking Sephora."

She cuts herself off before she mentions Olivia's other

online endeavors. She's babbling. It's because she's afraid of what Ms. Reddington is going to say. Something like *Emma, I'm so worried about you. Emma, you used to be such a good student. What's going on? Why are you saying these crazy things?*

Emma just wants to not answer any questions.

Ms. Reddington smiles and sits in the overstuffed armchair. "I'm good, thanks." Then her face grows serious. "I don't know if you're aware, but I knew your mother."

A pit opens up in Emma's stomach. All the words fall into it. This isn't what she thought Ms. Reddington was going to say at all. And just like the boy out on the quad, she has no idea how to handle it. "How did you know her?"

"We both went to Barnard. Not at the same time—she graduated ten years before me—but we were literature majors, and we had professors in common. We were part of an online alumni book group. We were reading all the great Russian novels."

"She never told me that." The sudden heaviness in Emma's stomach makes her feel almost physically ill. She had no idea that her mother was reading Dostoevsky in a book club. And maybe this exact detail doesn't truly matter, but it's yet another example of something she didn't know about her mom. She mentally adds it to the list of things she didn't know about Claire, wondering if anyone ever truly knows anyone else.

There are so many, many things she'll never know

unless someone else tells her, trusts her. And so many more things that Emma will *never know at all*.

"Why didn't you mention this three years ago, when I was in your class?" Emma asks.

"I don't know. I guess—I guess I was too scared to bring it up. She'd just…just passed, only six months before."

Emma says wryly, "You thought that maybe if you brought it up, suddenly I'd remember that my mother was dead? Like maybe I'd forgotten?"

Ms. Reddington flushes. "No, no, not that—"

"Sorry," Emma says. "That was rude. I get why you didn't mention it. And you're right. I was trying to keep it together. I *was* trying to forget."

"Losing a mother is terrible no matter when it happens," Ms. Reddington says. "But you were only a freshman. I can't even fathom it."

Emma watched her mother's face bloat from chemotherapy. She watched her hair fall out. Her steps grow uncertain. Her body grow more frail. And then, finally, less than a year after she was diagnosed, Emma watched her die.

Emma can't fathom it either, even though she lived through it.

Ms. Reddington leans forward and holds her hands in prayer position. "But what I came here to say, Emma, is that you have lost so much, but you have *so much more* to live for."

Emma's stomach hits rock bottom, and stays there. Ms.

Reddington was doing so well, and then she trotted out a cliché, something she might have picked up off a Brené Brown Pinterest board before coming to visit Emma. The truth is that Emma doesn't have so much to live for. In fact, she can't think of a single thing. And there are many, many good reasons to die.

But if she's going to make that happen, it's best to pretend that people are capable of changing her mind, and that she's listening.

"I still think about your essay on Elizabeth Bishop," Ms. Reddington says. "That's how good it was."

"'The art of losing isn't hard to master,'" Emma says, quoting the first line of Bishop's most famous poem. She looks hard at her teacher. "I don't agree with her, you know," she cries. "Art has nothing to do with it. It's just shitty luck and taking it on the chin."

"You're angry," Ms. Reddington says gently.

"Of course I am!" Emma says, not understanding how her teacher can treat such a simple statement as if it were an emotional breakthrough. "I'm sick and tired of losing members of my family!"

She gets up and starts pacing the room again. How much does a five-gallon canister of gas cost anyway? Twenty-five bucks for the gas, ten for the jug itself? If ordering from Uber Eats really did work, she'd have to leave a big tip, because that much gas would be heavy.

"Suffering is inevitable, but it is not evenly distributed," Ms. Reddington murmurs.

Emma ignores this; it is definitely not news.

Maybe she doesn't need that much gas after all. Maybe she only needs enough to get her clothes wet.

"The last time I talked to your mom, she told me a funny story about you," Ms. Reddington says. Emma's ears prick. "About the time you were in a dance performance, and you were supposed to dress up in your parents' clothes—"

Damn it, she's heard this story a thousand times. "And I was too little to understand that it was supposed to be funny," Emma says woodenly. "So when we got onstage and the audience started laughing, I started to cry. I was totally humiliated."

"But you kept on dancing, didn't you?" Ms. Reddington asks. "You were suffering, but *you kept on going.*"

Emma's surprised that an English teacher, of all people, would use a metaphor that blatantly obvious. And retro. Like the Energizer bunny.

But again: it's best to pretend she agrees.

"Yes," she says, nodding. "I just kept on going."

"Remember that," Ms. Reddington says urgently. "Remember that whenever you remember your mother." Her eyes start to glisten. "She was so proud of you. So, so proud. She knew that you were going to grow up to do great things, even if she wouldn't be around to see it."

Emma smiles at her old teacher, lips stretching tight over her teeth. She really is trying her best to help. She just doesn't have any idea what she's talking about.

I'm going to do a great thing, all right. But it means that I'm not going to grow up.

CHAPTER 27

AFTER MS. REDDINGTON leaves, Emma resumes her pacing. She wants to make another video, but she doesn't have her phone.

So she circles the room again and again, thinking about what to say once she gets it back. *The world's richest 1 percent own nearly half of the world's wealth. Two billion people live in countries where there's not enough water. Wildfires are raging in the Arctic Circle.*

She pauses by the window for a moment. Elliott and Aiden/Braydon/Caden have gone back to the dorms. The sun has slipped down behind the blue hills on the horizon, and the crickets chirp like crazy in the meadow. As Emma's standing there, the bell in Carter Tower rings, signaling quiet time on the Ridgemont campus.

Emma's mind is not quiet. *Never* quiet. Like an earworm, a chorus of bleak facts runs through her head. *Our oceans are dying. Suicide rates are climbing. Wars rage. Children starve.*

Claire is dead.

Claire is dead.

Claire is dead.

Of all the terrible truths, this is the most unbearable. Emma sinks to her knees and rests her head on the windowsill.

I could've handled all of it, Claire, if you would've just stayed alive.

Another knock—so gentle at first she thinks she imagines it—sounds on her door. Then she hears a voice that still makes her heart do a tiny leap inside her chest.

"Emma? It's Thomas. Can I come in?"

Emma doesn't answer right away. Now bittersweet memories are pushing aside all the bleak facts.

On the other side of the door is Thomas Takeda: senior, soccer star, student body VP, lead singer of Ridgemont's only rock band, and Emma's boyfriend from ninth grade until three months ago.

She saw him her very first night at Ridgemont, strumming his guitar in the dorm common room with half a dozen freshman girls sitting cross-legged at his feet, gazing up at him like they were daisies and he was the bright sun itself.

He had glossy black hair, thick black eyelashes, and long pianist's fingers. As he played and sang, he looked so relaxed and happy—like there was no better place on earth to be. Had Emma ever felt that way? If she had, she'd absolutely forgotten it.

Emma wanted to stay and listen to him sing, but she had no interest in joining his gaggle of admirers. Just before she turned to leave, Thomas looked up, caught her eye, and gave her the tiniest smile and a half shrug. As if he knew her already. Like they were in on some private joke: *Look at me,* he was saying, *taking song requests from fourteen-year-olds!*

Later, when she passed by his room, Thomas called out to her. "How come you didn't sing along to 'Watermelon Sugar'?"

Emma stopped, surprised by his teasing, challenging tone. "You already had plenty of backup singers, in case you hadn't noticed."

"Maybe," he'd acknowledged, looking up at her with an amused expression. "But your voice was the one I wanted to hear."

"Maybe play something better than Harry Styles next time."

Thomas Takeda, her first and last love. She'd miss him when she was gone.

"Em?" he's calling now. "Are you in there?"

Emma gets up slowly, like if she moves too quickly

she'll break. When she opens the door, Thomas immediately pulls her tight to his chest. His lips press against the top of her head, and she wants to melt into him. Wants to surrender. Wants him to take her away.

Doesn't want to die.

But that's impossible. She pulls back. His arms fall to his sides, and he stands awkwardly near the door, hands fidgeting with the hem of his shirt. "Babe," he says gently, "what's going on?"

Emma forces a grin. "Oh, nothing, I'm just having a sleepover in the admin building."

"Em, come on, it's me."

She sighs and sinks down onto the bed. "Fine. They're making me stay here because they don't trust me not to hurt myself. That's why Lori's out there standing guard."

Thomas lowers himself beside her. Close, but not close enough that their arms touch. He seems nervous, and she wonders if he's afraid for her—or afraid *of* her.

"It's been a while since we talked," he says. "It seems like things are..." He messes with his shirt some more. "It seems like things aren't going so great."

"No, they aren't," Emma says. "The whole world's falling apart, in case you hadn't noticed. They just declared this cute little bat extinct, did you see that? Meanwhile, flooding in Myanmar has killed hundreds if not thousands of people and animals. And teen girls are 'engulfed' in violence and trauma, the CDC says. Literally, that was the word they used. *Engulfed.*"

Thomas shifts his weight beside her. "Yeah, I try to avoid the news, I guess."

"But that's exactly the problem!" Emma cries. "How are we supposed to make things better when no one is willing to understand how bad they are to begin with?"

"I don't know, Emma," Thomas says, clearly unsettled. "I mean, yeah, we should try to improve things. But we're just kids. We don't run companies, and we don't make laws. Honestly, though, I'm more worried about you than I am about the state of the world."

"That's exactly the wrong take," Emma says. "My whole point is that we *have* to be worried about the state of the world. That's why I made the videos. They're a wake-up call."

"A wake-up call is one thing, but talking about setting yourself on fire is another!" he practically yells.

Wow, it's our first fight, Emma thinks.

"What's one less kid on the planet?" she says. "It's not like *teenagers* are going to go extinct."

"One less kid?" Thomas practically howls. "That's not how it works, Emma! You're not a number. You're a person!" He takes her hand and squeezes it. His voice goes very soft. "I mean, come on. When Claire died, is that what you told yourself? 'Well, there's one less person driving an SUV and eating meat and degrading the environment? One point for Planet Earth'?"

Emma sucks in her breath. His words feel like blows. What hurts more now—her arm or her heart? "That isn't fair," she says. "You can't turn it around like that."

"I'll do whatever I can to talk sense into you," Thomas says. His head drops. His shoulders hunch up, and for a second Emma thinks he might be crying. When he looks up at her, his cheeks are dry, but his expression is anguished.

"You've got to get real help," he goes on. "You've got to talk to someone. A shrink or whatever. And your friends. Me. I'm here for you, Em. You can tell me anything." His eyes search her face. His voice cracks as he says, "I still love you. You know that, right?"

Emma feels the sting of tears in her eyes. She didn't break up with Thomas because they fought or found out they were too different, or because of any of the other million reasons two people might pull away from each other. She just stopped being able to feel anything but despair. "You deserve someone happy," she said to him. "A nice, normal girl who laughs and play sports and does her homework and knows how to fall asleep at night. You don't want me."

She couldn't explain it to him, but she didn't feel like a person anymore. She was *anguish*, walking around in clothes.

"But I *do* want you," he insisted. "Nothing you do or say is going to change that."

She knew he meant it. Or at least thought he did. But for his own sake, she told him they were through.

Thomas's long, graceful fingers cover hers. "Em?" he says.

She pulls her hand away. She can't let him touch her. They don't live in the same world anymore. Thomas has a soccer scholarship to Stanford, whereas Emma is going to turn herself into ashes.

"I think you should go now," she says.

He doesn't want to, she can tell.

"I'm tired," she says. "I'm just going to go to sleep." She adds, "Lori's out there. She'll keep watch."

After Thomas reluctantly leaves, though, she doesn't sleep. She goes to the window, where the moon floats above the quad like a great white eye. The campus is quiet, and she is alone. The world is still dying, and Claire is still dead.

Why would she want to stay here?

CHAPTER 28

The day before the fire

THE SMELL OF fresh pancakes is nauseating.

Or maybe Emma feels sick to her stomach because everyone in the Ridgemont dining hall is staring at her. *This* is why she's been avoiding the place. *This* is why she's been surviving on cold Pop-Tarts and Lärabars.

Some kids try to be subtle about it—Zadie from French class sneaks glances out of the corners of her sly green eyes—but most gawk openly.

"For seventy-five grand a year, you'd think they could get some decent chairs around here," mutters Emma's father, shifting around uncomfortably in his seat. "It's like sitting on a pile of kindling."

Byron Blake arrived at Ridgemont Academy after getting a call from Thomas last night, and his thundering voice awakened Emma from her half sleep. *This is no way to treat my daughter! She's coming with me!*

"I don't think they designed the chairs with a six-foot-five man in mind," Emma says quietly.

Byron's head swivels as he scans the room. In his custom black suit, he looks like a rich, pissed-off undertaker. "A lot of ninety-pound weaklings around here."

"Dad!" Emma exclaims. "Don't be rude."

"The truth is never rude," Byron says. He glares at his pancakes before cutting the whole stack in half with a violent slice of his knife. "Undercooked," he mutters.

Emma sighs. She's glad he rescued her from solitary confinement. But that doesn't mean she wants to sit here, hair unbrushed, wearing the sweats she slept in, and eat pancakes with him. He's always been gruff, but his roughness and impatience have only gotten worse since her mother's death. And then, when Claire died...

"The bacon's too fatty," he says.

Emma bites her tongue. Slowly butters a piece of toast she doesn't feel like eating.

Then Byron looks up from his breakfast and trains his eyes on Emma, his gaze sharp and probing. "I don't appreciate what you're doing," he says. "This supposed cry for help—it's nonsense. I know that, and so do you."

They're tucked away in a corner, but Emma can feel everyone's eyes on them. She pushes her thumb into the burn on her arm. The sudden flare of pain somehow reassures her. It reminds her of what's at stake.

"I agree," Emma says. "If it were a cry for help, it would be nonsense. But I'm not asking for help." She locks eyes with her father. "Everyone seems to think I need it. But I don't."

"How's your arm?" Byron asks. As if he knows what she's doing right now.

Emma stops pressing on the bandage. "It still hurts."

"That was an interesting experiment," he says.

Emma nods. There's a sudden lump in her throat, and she doesn't know why.

Maybe it's all the things she won't ever say to him. *Daddy, why didn't you save Claire? Daddy, we're all alone. Daddy, I can't take it any longer—*

She feels like she might start choking.

She stands up. "I'm going to go get some more water."

When Emma comes back to the table with a plastic pitcher of ice water, her father is frowning and stripping the fat from his bacon. She wants to take him by his broad, strong shoulders and shake him. *Don't you understand what's going on?* Instead she sits down, leans forward so their faces are almost touching, and says quietly, "Were Claire's cries for help not loud enough?"

Her father looks away. His entire posture changes, the

muscles in his jaw twitching. With nothing to complain about and no one else to blame, the man has nothing to say. In the silence between them, the whispers grow louder.

"I knew she was hurting," Emma says. "But I had no idea how much. Did you?"

Slowly Byron shakes his head. "I didn't know," he says finally. "I didn't know." But then he looks straight at Emma. His two hands have become fists. "She was different, Emma. She wasn't like us."

"Wasn't *like* us? What do you mean?"

"I'm tough," he says. "And you're tough. Claire was strong, but she was a china teacup compared to you. You're the toughest person I know. You're made of iron. You're going to be fine. You just need something to do, something to keep you busy, take your mind off it."

Her father might be able to stay busy and not feel things, to work until all of his thoughts only flow through one channel, a desensitized, unfeeling one. He is never still, her father.

His hands are flexing, fingernails digging into his palms or darting out to rearrange silverware. Even here, on his mercy mission to save the only daughter he has left, he's multitasking, putting the tines of his fork at a perfect angle to his plate, refolding the linen napkin into a more perfect triangle. Anything to stay busy. Anything to flood his mind with something other than emotion.

Emma isn't like that. Emma feels things, right down to her core. She feels the loss not only of her own mother and sister, but of every elephant that died for its tusks, and the pain that comes from watching the uptick of the thermometer each summer. Emma wants to direct all her efforts toward what she feels, until she's able to do something that makes other people wake up and feel that way too.

But she can't admit that to him. Even if she did, he wouldn't believe her. Byron Blake says she's tough, that she's going to be fine, and Byron Blake is always right.

CHAPTER 29

EMMA'S FATHER GLIDES off in a chauffeured Lincoln Navigator soon after breakfast. He waves as the car pulls onto the road, his phone already pinned to his ear.

Emma lifts a hand in return. "Goodbye," she whispers as the car grows smaller in the distance. "Have a nice life. Or at least, a busy one."

She really hopes he will. He'll remarry, of course. Some tanned, young tennis-playing blonde, a daughter of Boston high society. Someone who stays equally busy with her garden club and Orangetheory classes. Someone who will be content with things looking like they're perfect and not care how they actually are. Maybe he'll even have more kids. He's only forty-six—he's got plenty of time.

She wonders if he'll figure out, next round, that maximizing billable hours isn't the best parenting strategy. That money is so much less important than he thinks it is. Success, too, for that matter. She wonders if he'll figure out that pouring himself into work won't save anyone—not even him.

Probably not. As the saying goes, a leopard doesn't change its spots.

Amur leopards are on the brink of extinction.

Emma turns and goes back to her dorm room. Olivia's blasting Taylor Swift and checking her outfit in the full-length mirror. She's wearing a halter top, baggy low-rise jeans, and black platform Converses, just like every other day. Her skin is dewy and perfect.

"Hey, Liv." Emma slips into faded Levi's and a rumpled white button-down.

Olivia whirls around to face her. "Oh, my god, Emma! Your phone's been blowing *up*! Where were you last night? Did you sneak out? Were you with a guy? Did you and Thomas get back together?"

Emma almost laughs. Her roommate's the *one* person on campus who doesn't know what's going on. She's probably spent 90 percent of her time online since Emma posted her video, but the most important part of social media to her is the *me.* Emma doubts she even looks at her feed or anyone else's posts; she just goes straight to her latest, looking for likes and new follows. Or, if it's her OnlyFans, her account balance. A better name for her would be Oblivia.

"I spent the night in the nurse's office," Emma finally says. "I thought I was coming down with something."

Olivia takes a quick step away from her, covering her mouth and nose with a manicured hand.

"Don't worry," Emma says. "I'm not contagious."

And I'm not—high anxiety coupled with a feeling of dread is not something she can pass on to someone else. But awareness, and making sure everyone has all the facts? That's a virus she can create, and hope that it burns through the population.

When she picks up her phone, she sees 232 new texts. Classmates—neighbors—cousins she hasn't seen in years: everyone's writing. They beg to know what's going on, urge her to text them back, or tell her in all caps, DON'T DO IT.

Is yr dad gone? writes Jade. Call me NOW.

Thomas writes, lunch—meet me at the field LY.

"LY" stands for "love you."

She's about to read a text from Elliott when the battery dies.

"Shit," Emma says.

"Everything okay?" Olivia asks as she brushes her long, soft hair.

No, Olivia, everything is not okay. Would you like me to tell you all the ways in which everything is fucked?

"Yeah, totally." Emma slides her computer out of her backpack. "Have you seen my phone charger? Or my computer cord?"

Olivia shakes her head, watching the effect in the mirror as her perfect curls toss.

Emma realizes that the cops probably took them, just in case she considered strangling herself with one of them.

She opens her laptop. Her battery is at 35 percent, and her heart is pounding. Time to see how far her message has reached.

She clicks over to her second YouTube video, which she reposted under a new account a mere hour after Mr. Hastings made her take it down. The views are staggering. In disbelief, Emma scrolls down through hundreds of comments. A lot of people are urging her to get help. Others are offering her matches.

You're an inspiration, writes GalaxieStar.

I wish i was brave as u, says tommyboy09.

Get outta here while you can.

Will u be my gf?

I feel u bae—i'm catchin the bus too.

Emma doesn't know what "catching the bus" means, but she thinks it's funny that some random person called her "bae."

A charger drops with a clunk on Emma's desk. "Here," Olivia says, "use mine."

"Thanks," Emma says woodenly. She plugs in her phone and watches as it comes back to life.

Another text comes in with a ding. It's from a number she doesn't recognize. Google emma on fire, it says.

CHAPTER 30

EMMA ON FIRE

Teen announces self-immolation intention

Odell, NH
April 14, 2025
by Rachel Daley, special to the Boston Globe

Yesterday morning, I met the girl whose name is on the lips of concerned parents, climate activists, and teenage influencers alike: Emma Blake.

Unless you live under an actual rock, you know her name too. She's the seventeen-year-old Ridgemont Academy junior who's pledged to self-immolate in protest of the state of the world.

I met Emma in her dorm room as campus police searched her drawers for items she might be able to use for self-harm. Her dark eyes had a haunted quality, the unmistakable mark of sleepless nights and a heart burdened by more than it should ever have to bear.

Emma politely but firmly declined to discuss her plans on the record. A far cry from the impassioned, defiant girl in her videos, in person she was guarded and cautious, her words carefully chosen and few in number. Her reluctance to speak left me wondering about the girl behind the viral sensation. Who is she, really, when the camera isn't rolling?

The Internet is divided about Emma, her self-proclaimed sacrifice sparking both admiration and apprehension. There's no question her video has shaken up the digital world, but what is it that's driving her?

Is she a martyr for a generation that has come of age in a world fraught with conflict and dread—a beacon of radical activism willing to sacrifice herself for change?

Or—and this strikes me as more likely—is she a troubled young girl, a teen grappling with deep-seated depression like so many of our young people, her pain hijacked and amplified by the megaphone of social media?

And who are we, as a nation and a world, that our children make declarations such as hers?

CHAPTER 31

"I JUST LEFT her. She's fine," Byron says brusquely.

Hastings presses his lips into a thin line. *Fine* is hardly the word he'd use for Emma. What was it she said in that awful video? *We're at the brink of total disaster. Everything is going wrong.* He can't exactly argue that she's wrong, at this point. "Have you read the *Boston Globe* article? We can't let—"

"That woman will be out of a job by EOD," Byron says. "So just listen to me. You can't lock up my daughter. It's technically kidnapping. And you can't keep her phone and laptop away from her either. She's protesting, and you're interfering with her freedom of speech."

Hastings grits his teeth. "I understand your argument," he says, not mentioning that the man has just threatened

Rachel Daley's job, essentially taking away her freedom of speech. But he's dealt with the überrich his whole life—he knows the rules apply only where they want them to. He picks up his coffee cup and then sets it back down again, debating his words. "But this isn't about Emma's constitutional rights; it's about her welfare."

"Are you suggesting that I'm not concerned about her welfare? What Emma needs right now is stability. Consistency. Removing her from school, from her friends, is going to take away one of the few things my daughter has left."

And his daughter is the only thing he has left. Could that be a touch of vulnerability in Byron's voice? But it doesn't even matter. The man refuses to believe that his daughter is a danger to herself.

"We're in uncharted territory, Mr. Blake, and I can't let Ridgemont be the setting for a tragedy."

"It won't be," Byron says. "Jesus Christ, are you not around enough teenage girls to understand how they act? She's being dramatic, sure. But I know my daughter better than you ever will, and I would never let anything bad happen to her. So you need to—"

But Hastings has had just about enough. Byron might as well have tossed out the word *hysteria,* the way he's dismissing teenage girls—half of the student population whose well-being Hastings is responsible for. "Sorry, what?" he says. "Mr. Blake? You're cutting out!"

This time it's the headmaster who hangs up on the lawyer. Peregrine Hastings feels adrenaline rushing through his veins.

I can't believe I just did that.

It feels so good, he wishes he could go back in time and do it again. Actually, if he could go back in time, there are a lot of things he would change, starting with paying attention to Emma's mental state when she came to Ridgemont after her mother died, and monitoring her more closely when Claire committed suicide.

But since he can't go back in time, Hastings has to figure out what to do next.

Tick tick tick goes the big black grandfather clock that once belonged to Edgar Ridgemont. It's the day before the fire—that's what Emma said. Time is running out.

CHAPTER 32

BY LUNCHTIME HASTINGS has convened eight members of the Ridgemont board in an emergency meeting. The school's lawyer, George Forbes, is also there, pink in the face from an early-morning tennis game. Fiona orders sandwiches from the local deli, which sit untouched in the middle of the conference table.

After thanking everyone for being available on such short notice, Hastings presents the issue to the Ridgemont brain trust. "I wish we were here under happier circumstances," he says. "But as some of you may be aware, we have a student making public threats of self-harm. Her name is Emma Blake, she's a junior, and she wants to bring attention to the world's problems by burning herself alive."

Monica Zoller, founder of a multimillion-dollar real

estate firm, audibly gasps. So does Robert Bass III, scion of a sports equipment empire.

Hastings swallows nervously. "She's made a video, which she posted on YouTube, in which she states her intention to set herself on fire." He swallows again. "Here on the Ridgemont campus."

The room erupts in noise, and Hastings lifts his hand to quiet the board. "We had the video taken down, but it has been reposted countless times. Students at schools like ours, in particular, are taking notice. A climate march at Boyden descended into vandalism of the student union. At Kingsley there's a student who's on a hunger strike."

"But no one else is saying they're going to burn themselves alive," George says quickly. "Activism is one thing. Threatening suicide is another."

Bryce Knode, a Harvard engineer, speaks up from a Zoom screen. "How seriously do you take this young woman's threat?"

"Very," says Hastings. "Emma's father, on the other hand, insists that she's fine."

I know my daughter much better than you do, he said. *If I believed Emma was actually in danger, I'd be there by lunchtime.* Well, Byron Blake did come to Ridgemont—and then he left again, an hour later, cell phone pressed to his ear.

"Does Emma have a history of mental illness?" Monica wants to know.

"No, according to her father," Hastings says. "But her sister did. She committed suicide in December. And Emma's mother died of cancer right before she enrolled at Ridgemont."

His words fall like stones in the room.

Clarabelle Porter, Ridgemont '72, lifts her sagging, aristocratic chin. "That poor, remarkable girl," she says, fingering the pearls at her neck. "I can only imagine the pain she must be feeling right now."

"It's terrible, I agree. We need to help her, but what is the best course of action?" Hastings says. "I need your counsel. I think she should be removed from campus immediately, and taken someplace where she can be under constant surveillance. But her father, who is a major donor, has threatened a lawsuit. He says that Emma is merely exercising her right to free speech." He loosens his tie. The room is unbearably hot. "And Emma would argue that she's exercising her right to social protest."

"It doesn't sound like social protest," Monica says. "It sounds like depression and suicidal ideation."

"We aren't qualified to diagnose her," Hastings says. "The question is what to do with her. We've suspended students for dangerous behaviors before. We've sent students in crisis to the psychiatric hospital. And we've put other students on leaves of absence when we felt that was the best course of action." He removes his jacket. There's no relief. "But in every instance prior, we had the assistance and the support of the student's parents. In this case, we have a father who very clearly states that his daughter must stay in school, or he'll sue."

The ticking of the grandfather clock drills into Hastings's ears as he waits for someone to say something.

"Ridgemont isn't equipped to handle this particular situation," George Forbes says. "Nor should we be asked to, for moral, ethical, and legal reasons."

"And we have to remember, this is about more than just one troubled student," says Ed Jensen, a hedge fund manager, from his little Zoom box. "This is about the safety of everyone here."

"But a lawsuit?" says Dominic Chadwick shyly. He's barely out of Cornell, the youngest member of the board, and Hastings has always found him timid and dull. "I assume we don't want that?"

"We also don't want a girl burning herself to death," says Monica flatly.

"What if her dad's right, though?" Dominic goes on. "What if he knows her best?"

Hastings sighs. "I think that parents sometimes believe what they want to believe. Byron Blake in particular is very accustomed to being right. And maybe he is. But I'm not sure that's a risk we should take."

"I'll be frank. I can't imagine her doing it," says Robert Bass III.

"But it's better to be safe than sorry," George says.

Hastings looks around the room. He understands that no one *wants* to believe Emma's threats are real. But that doesn't mean they aren't.

And while no one will say it out loud, they want to protect Ridgemont's reputation in addition to protecting Emma Blake's life.

"I believe she needs to be hospitalized immediately," Hastings says. "Are we in agreement?"

"I'll drive her myself," Monica says.

"No," George says. "We'll call an ambulance."

Hastings looks at all of them in turn. They're nodding. Some are frowning; a few are looking offscreen, multitasking while discussing a teenage girl's looming self-immolation. But he has a consensus, and he's going to run with it.

"Fiona," he barks. "Call NH Hospital."

CHAPTER 33

WHEN EMMA EMERGES onto the quad, the spring breeze cools her burning cheeks. Hundreds of thousands of people—more, even—have heard her message. They think she's brave. They think she's heroic. They think she's doing the right thing.

It's what she wanted.

So why doesn't it feel good?

The Boston Globe *article,* says the small, bitter voice Emma knows so well. *That know-it-all reporter.*

She barely said two words to Rachel Daley, and then Rachel turned it into an article questioning Emma's sanity and motives.

A troubled young girl, a teen grappling with deep-seated depression. Emma stomps across the grass. Maybe Rachel should lose a few of her precious "touchy" sisters and see how she feels. Maybe she would find out what happens when the only two people who ever tried to take care of her vanish from the face of the earth forever.

Maybe if Rachel could feel what it is like to truly be alone, then she'd understand.

Suddenly Emma stops in the middle of the green expanse. Her skin feels electric. A shiver runs up her spine.

They're all watching me, even now.

Ridgemont students looking out of windows. Professors leaning in classroom doorways. The campus police trailing at a safe, respectable distance.

It's like she's onstage. She's the star of a one-woman show called *Will She Do It?* And no one knows if it's a comedy or a tragedy until she strikes a flame.

CHAPTER 34

HASTINGS AND MONICA Zoller, the mother of two teen girls herself, hurry across campus, hoping to find Emma. She's been skipping a lot of classes, but Hastings knows she never misses French, and he wants to catch her before the bell rings. The fewer Ridgemont students who see her being escorted to a waiting ambulance, the better.

He's asked Fiona to call Thomas Takeda, though. If Emma resists going to the hospital, Thomas might be able to help persuade her. Thomas is a good kid. A sane kid. He knows her better than anyone else at Ridgemont, and he definitely doesn't want her to die.

On their way to Doyle Hall, the humanities building, Hastings and Monica pass clusters of twelfth graders dotting the verdant grass of the quad. They all have independent study after lunch, which in the spring basically means free time. Hastings resists his habit of asking them if they're using their time wisely. Their acceptance letters from Stanford and Yale and Notre Dame and Duke are probably on the way. The sun is shining. Why on earth should they study?

Hastings and Monica have turned down a path beneath one of the dorms when something white catches Hastings's eye. He looks up to the dorm's second story. There's a tattered bedsheet hanging down between two windows.

EMMA'S RIGHT, it says.

As he watches, another sheet unfurls, its letters scrawled in spray paint red as blood.

WE'RE BURNING ALREADY

"Oh dear," Monica breathes.

Hastings's speed increases to a jog. "Make them take those down!" he calls over his shoulder. "I'm going to find Emma."

But when Hastings, breathless, arrives outside room 119, Emma isn't there. Her friend Jade, who normally sits next to her in French class, hasn't seen her since breakfast.

"I'll text her again," Jade says, eyes dark with concern. "I've been texting her all morning."

"And she hasn't gotten back to you?" Hastings tries to keep his tone even. Outside, he hears a group cheer from the seniors on the green. Someone must have unfurled another banner. Some of the French students go to the window, peering out.

"No," Jade says. "She's not answering. Are you…are you worried?"

Hastings takes a deep breath, puts his hands on her shoulders. He's seen teenagers act like they can handle everything, but over the years he's learned that when something serious happens, they still look to an adult. *They're still children,* he thinks. *Why can't Byron Blake see that?*

"Everything is going to be fine," he tells Jade. "Please keep trying to reach her."

In the hallway, Hastings runs into Thomas Takeda. "She's not there?" Thomas asks, craning his neck toward room 119.

"No," Hastings says, hating himself for thinking she would be. Why would a girl who intends to set herself on fire still go to French class?

"Maybe she's in her room?"

"That's where we're going," Hastings says. "See if you can find out when and where someone saw her last."

Hastings hurries on ahead, with Thomas tapping at his phone behind him. He jogs down another path, through the lilac grove, and then they're at Emma's dorm. He's pulling open the front door when he hears the ambulance siren.

Idiots! He *specifically* said no siren. He didn't want to bring any extra attention to the situation.

As Hastings hustles down the hall, he's surprised to find himself praying. *Just be there, Emma, just be there.*

He yanks open her door without knocking. Stumbles over the edge of her ugly pink rug and nearly falls into the room.

It's empty.

His shoulders slump, his stomach drops.

Thomas comes in behind him, still looking down at his phone. "Spencer Jenkins says he saw Emma leaving campus, Mr. Hastings."

"When?" The word can barely get out between his clenched teeth.

"Before first period."

That was over three hours ago.

An ambulance can't take away a girl it can't find.

And he can't protect a girl who doesn't want to be found.

CHAPTER 35

WEARING COMFORTABLE SNEAKERS and carrying a light backpack, Emma makes good time. It's a four-mile walk to the Circle K, the gas station where Ridgemont kids with cars come for frozen pizzas and Monster Energy drinks and NoDoz during finals week. Where the ones with fake IDs can sometimes walk out with a case of Bud tallboys, depending on who's working the register.

Emma grabs a bottle of Starbucks cold brew and goes up to the counter. "Do you sell gas cans?"

The guy looks up from his phone. He's probably nineteen, with jet-black dyed hair and sunken cheeks. He looks like someone who never goes outside. "Yeah," he says. "How many you need?"

"Is it something people usually buy a lot of?"

He shrugs. "Not really. But the boss says I ought to encourage everyone to buy more of everything." He rubs two fingers together, like he's feeling invisible money. "Why get a six-pack when you can get a case? Why one cold brew when you can have two?"

"I just need one gas can."

"They're in the back. Hang on."

When he comes back, he's got a small red plastic can. "We're out of the big ones. This'll hold two gallons. That work?"

Emma figures it will. "How much does a gallon of gas weigh, do you think?"

"No idea."

Emma thinks back to chemistry class. "Water's eight point three pounds per gallon. Gas is lighter, I know that." Emma taps a finger on the counter. "I wonder if I should get lighter fluid too..."

He peers at her. "Do I know you?" he asks.

Emma starts. Then quickly she shakes her head. "No," she says. "I'm not from around here. I ran out of gas back on Route 12. Stupid fuel gauge is broken—"

"You look really familiar," he says.

She puts a fifty-dollar bill on the counter. "I'm going to pump my gas now. I think this should cover everything." She straightens her shoulders and walks calmly but quickly out of the store. She can feel his eyes on the back of her neck.

Of course he's seen you before. He probably lives online.

Just...hurry.

She fumbles with the gas nozzle and dribbles gas on her shoes, but she manages to fill the can with a gallon of gas. She wants it to be easy to carry, and it's not like she needs that much. She puts the canister in her backpack, nestling it next to her phone and her toiletries bag. That's when she hears him calling after her.

"Emma!" he shouts. "You're Emma On Fire!" He's coming out of the store, waving at her. "Your videos are *sick*!"

Is that a compliment? Does it even matter?

Emma doesn't wave back, doesn't ask him what he means. She starts running.

CHAPTER 36

THE GAS CAN slams against Emma's back all the way to the intersection, her backpack gurgling. She hangs a left on Poplar Street, and then she finally slows down and tries to catch her breath. An old man watering his pansies looks disapprovingly at her. She's sweaty and wild-eyed, and suddenly she feels like an idiot. Did she really think the cashier was going to *chase* her? He probably hasn't run since the day he discovered Nintendo, and anyway, he couldn't leave the Slim Jims and the beer cases unattended. All he could do was shout after her, *I know you!*

And isn't that the point? Two YouTube videos, seen millions of times, and now she's a celebrity in Nowheresville, New Hampshire, and probably everywhere else people have TikTok and 5G. Her message has exploded. She's officially gone viral. She should feel triumphant. But instead she feels scared. There's a flickering of emotion running under her skin. She wanted an audience, now she has one.

She can't let them down.

Thankfully no one at the Creekside Motel has any idea about Emma on Fire, which is how she's able to rent a room with Claire's ID ("Jocelyn Peters") and $400 in cash as a security deposit.

"Ice is between rooms fifteen and sixteen, hon," says the old lady at the front desk, smiling sweetly with tobacco-stained teeth. "Right next to the vending machine."

"Thanks."

Emma already knows where the ice is. Byron, when he visited Claire at all, refused to spend the night, saying that the Wi-Fi at Creekside was too slow. But her mom was charmed by the small rooms painted a faded pink. She enjoyed making an adventure of staying overnight, bringing along a bottle of Château Lafite Rothschild and sparkling cider for Emma. She'd pour the drinks into the motel's little plastic cups and make a toast.

"Quiet time after ten," the woman says. She narrows her eyes. "And no guests."

"You got it," Emma says, taking the key. She knows at least six Ridgemont students who lost their virginity at the Creekside. Her plans don't include that, not by a long shot.

Her room's decor is familiar. Tossing her backpack onto

the bed, she goes into the tiny bathroom, strips off her clothes, and climbs into the shower. She runs the water so hot, it feels like her skin's going to blister. She has to hold her injured arm out of the way, because hot water on a burn feels like molten lava.

After her shower, Emma sits on the bed and takes out her phone. Her home screen is nothing but notifications. Ten messages from Jade. Eight from Thomas. Four missed calls from a Ridgemont number. Emma ignores them all. Instead she opens TikTok and searches #emmaonfire.

There are thousands of videos. Her words have become sound bites for lip-syncers. "We keep cramming more and more people onto the planet, and guess what," mouths a baby Goth with a septum piercing, "news flash, you guys—it *isn't getting any bigger.*" Other people post reaction videos or offer up depressing facts of their own. "Human sperm counts have fallen by fifty percent in the last fifty years," shouts a middle-aged man in a baseball cap. "It's because we're polluted, man! Soon we won't even be able to make more humans!" A teenage guy from Ottawa has autotuned her voice and put it to a beat.

Some people talk about how right she is, how *brave,* while others claim her videos are just a desperate cry for attention. Which is ironic, Emma thinks, because the entire TikTok platform is a cry for attention. One video—six million views—puts her face on a marshmallow that's being roasted over a campfire. There's even a dance in which people of all ages do a series of haunting, flickering hand movements set to a remix of the chorus of "I'm On Fire."

Emma lets her phone drop to the floor and falls backward on the flowered comforter. *You're supposed to be talking about the world's problems!* she wants to scream. *You're not supposed to be dancing to a conveniently relevant Bruce Springsteen song or roasting my face on a fucking Jet-Puffed!*

How did her message get so distorted?

After a while she grabs her phone again. Of course the stupid reactions are the ones she saw first—they're the lowest common denominator. Surely somewhere out there, someone is taking her intentions seriously? She has to find out.

Another text comes in. It's from a number she doesn't know, but for some reason she opens it. There's no message, just a cell phone video. A bunch of kids outside a high school wave signs and chant. The sound quality's terrible, so she has to watch it a few times before she understands what they're saying.

Save Emma. Save the world. Save Emma. Save the world.

CHAPTER 37

THEY DON'T GET it either. Emma doesn't want to be "saved."

But at least they've got the world part right. *Yes, try to save the world,* she thinks. *I'll be cheering for you from...wherever I am.*

Protests, texts this unknown person. Marches. Happening because of *you.*

Emma puts her phone back on the bedside table. *This* is what she wanted. She feels charged now. Electric. She knows she's making a difference. Her death, unlike Claire's, will mean something.

So now she can do what? Relax?

How is a person supposed to relax on the last night of their life?

The suicide rate for people ages twenty to twenty-four increased 63 percent from 2001 through 2021.

The global rich have more than they could ever consume, while a billion people struggle to get enough to eat.

She reaches for the remote. She'll find a stupid movie and stare at it until her brain goes numb. But instead her attention gets pulled to the fake watercolor on the wall, which shows a little yellow cottage beside a white picket fence. On the other side of the fence, six puffy sheep dot a bright green meadow.

She realizes that she's in the same room she shared with her mother when they came for Claire's graduation.

Emma was ten years old, too tall and too bookish already. Back then she couldn't stop talking about going to Ridgemont herself. She was a walking brochure for the place. "Ridgemont Academy has an eight-to-one student-to-teacher ratio. The percentage of teachers holding an advanced degree is eighty-six. There are forty-five US states and territories represented in the student body, and thirty-eight countries. There are over a hundred student clubs and organizations on campus."

Her mother, usually so patient, snapped at her. "Can't you lay off the *facts* for a night? I haven't slept in weeks!"

Emma blinked back tears as she sat next to her parents, listening to Claire's valedictory speech about the importance of perseverance and having high expectations for yourself.

"When things get hard," Claire told the assembled crowd, "you must not give up. When I felt like I couldn't do any more homework, or any more violin practicing, or any more sprints, I'd say to myself, 'What's the matter? It's only *pain.*' And pain, like my dad always told us, 'is weakness leaving the body.'"

"That's my girl," Byron whispered.

That night they ate a celebratory steak dinner in Concord. Then Claire headed back to the dorms, and Byron went back to Cambridge, and it was just Emma and her mother in the little pink motel room. By tradition, her mother pulled a bottle of Château Lafite Rothschild and a bottle of sparkling cider from her suitcase and filled up two of the motel's plastic cups.

Then Sarah Blake drained one cup and quickly poured herself another. Emma had never seen her mother drink more than half a glass of wine at a dinner party. She didn't look like she was celebrating anymore.

"Mom?" Emma asked. "Do you want some water?"

"It isn't easy," Sarah said, almost to herself. "No, in fact it's very hard."

"What is?" Emma asked, suddenly worried.

Her mother shook her head. Took another gulp of wine. Stared dully at the watercolor sheep, which she said looked like wads of Kleenex with legs.

"Mom?" Emma scooted closer to her on the bed. "What's so hard?"

"It's hard to be the kind of person your father wants us to be," Sarah said. "I've done it for twenty years, and I'm very, very tired."

Little flares of alarm were going off inside Emma, but she didn't know what to say or do. She was only in fourth grade. She reached for her mother's hand. She said, helplessly, "Everything's going to be okay!"

Her mother had laughed tonelessly, the sound harsh and low in the small room. "Of course everything is going to be okay, sweetheart. You're going to go to Ridgemont. Your sister is going to Harvard. Your dad will continue to make more money than we can spend, and I'll…I'll…"

She'd waved her hand in the air, eyes cloudy with confusion.

"I'll just keep being Mrs. Byron Blake."

And her mother turned to Emma and put her hand against her cheek. Then she forced herself to smile. "But there will be good times for us, my dear, of course. So many of them."

But Sarah Blake was dead less than four years later, so really, how many more good times did she get?

CHAPTER 38

"IT ISN'T FAIR," Emma says out loud. "She deserved better."

And so did Claire.

But maybe the idea of deserving anything at all is meaningless. Do babies born today deserve to grow up in a world of war and hunger, mental illness and loneliness, hurricanes and deforestation? They don't ask to be born in the first place, and they *definitely* don't ask to be born in the middle of worldwide crises.

Emma wishes, with every molecule in her body, that she could still talk to Claire the way she used to.

"Oh, Claire," Emma says to the empty, anonymous room. "Why did you have to go?" She shakes her head. "But you didn't *have* to. You chose to. And I will never understand why."

Once again, Emma can't sit still. As she paces, she keeps

talking out loud, because hearing her voice makes her feel less alone. It's almost like she can imagine the words somehow reaching Claire, wherever she is. She barely notices the tears streaming down her cheeks.

"No one understands why I'm making my choice either. But if I'm honest, Claire, I think part of me was never sure that I was going to go through with it. Like maybe it'd be enough to raise all those issues and make that terrible threat." She shoves her hands into the pockets of her jeans. Finds a lone Tic Tac, which she tosses into the corner. The room needs a good vacuuming anyway. "Not that the whole thing was an empty threat from the start. But I guess I thought there was a chance that I could, like, talk the talk but not have to walk the walk." She laughs awkwardly. "God, I sound like our PE teacher. Mr. Briggs. You never had him. He only speaks in clichés. 'You miss one hundred percent of the shots you don't take,' and stuff like that. It's so dumb.

"But now I'm getting distracted. I guess what I'm saying, Claire, is that this whole thing has gotten so much bigger than me. People are paying attention, just like I wanted them to. They're marching and having rallies. They're making videos and calling for change. So suddenly it feels like there's no way I can back down." She pauses in front of the sheep painting. It really is ugly. "I won't miss *that*," she says. "There's a lot of things I won't miss, I guess. So maybe there's a bright side to having to burn myself alive."

CHAPTER 39

THE RINGING OF Emma's phone startles her back to reality. Glancing at the screen, she recognizes the number as the same one the texts came from. She wipes her eyes. Picks up. "Who is this?"

"Emma, this is Rachel Daley."

Anger floods Emma's body. "What could you possibly want from me? You've already got your story, even if it was bullshit—"

"Emma, I'm sorry," the reporter interrupts. "What you read is not the story I turned in. It's the story my editor wanted to tell."

"I don't believe you."

"I'll send you my original version."

"Don't bother. Good—"

"Emma, wait," Rachel says. "Don't hang up. Please." Emma can hear her take a deep breath. "I know how alone you feel right now. The world is watching you, yes, but they don't understand you."

Emma scoffs. "And you do?"

"I feel your anger," Rachel says urgently. "I know the world's in trouble, and I'm not interested in pretending that it isn't. That's why I became a reporter! That's why I wanted to cover your story. Have you read any of my pieces? Last week I wrote about how the ocean around Cape Cod is warming faster than nearly any in the world. The week before, I wrote about Massachusetts being one of nine states to sue the oil and gas companies for—"

"I get it," Emma says.

"But that doesn't mean that I don't think you're hurting," Rachel says quietly. "*You*, Emma Blake. It doesn't mean that I don't think you're in trouble, too, as much as the world is."

Emma stiffens. "This isn't about me."

"But it *is*," Rachel says. "Look, I don't want you to do this. But I can't stop you."

Emma looks over at the gas can. In the pocket of her backpack the heirloom Zippo waits. "No one can," she says.

"Do you know what they say is the difference between being a suicide and being a martyr?" Rachel asks.

"No."

"Press coverage," Rachel says flatly.

Emma stiffens. What a terrible thing to say. But it's true, isn't it? *I'm not going to be the girl who burned and no one knew why.*

"So if you're set on doing it, let me be there," Rachel says.

It takes Emma a moment to speak. "Are you saying that you *want* to see me actually set myself on fire?"

"Emma," Rachel says, "I'm saying—"

But Emma hangs up. She's heard enough. Rachel Daley might talk the talk when it comes to caring for the planet, but the only walk she wants to walk is the one that gets her above the fold on the front page. If that means a great shot of Emma's skin sliding off her bones, so be it.

"Can you believe this shit?" she asks the empty room, asks Claire.

But then she realizes that there is someone she needs to talk to, someone who needs to believe some other shit that is very, very real.

CHAPTER 40

"EMMA!" BYRON'S VOICE booms onto the line. "You caught me on my way to a meeting."

He sounds happy to hear from her, which isn't a given. He hates to be interrupted at work, even by his beloved and now only daughter.

"We have to talk," Emma says.

"But we just did," he says. "We had breakfast together this morning, remember?"

"You said some words, and then I said some words. Don't pretend it was a meaningful conversation."

Byron sucks in his breath sharply. Emma's never spoken to him like this.

"You keep insisting that what I'm saying isn't true," Emma says. "You seem incapable of taking me seriously.

And you did the same thing to Claire. She told you she was hurting. And you kept telling her that she was strong, that she was doing great, that she could handle anything life threw at her. But she couldn't."

"She could have handled it," Byron insists. "She's not like—"

"You and me?" Emma interrupts. "Her death proves that she couldn't. And everything I've been saying lately proves that I can't either."

"It only proves she gave up too soon," Byron says. "And your behavior lately is nothing more than an outpouring of grief, another version of pain and weakness leaving the body."

"You don't get it, do you?" Emma cries. "She was grieving. She felt completely alone. We weren't there for her." Emma feels tears sliding down her cheeks. "If we'd listened better—if we'd really understood how bad things were—then maybe she'd still be here."

"It was Claire's decision," Byron says quietly. "If I could change it—" His voice breaks. "I would give anything. I thought losing your mother was hard. And it was. It was awful. But losing Claire almost killed me."

"You didn't even take a week off of work!" Emma yells.

"My work was the only thing keeping me alive!" he shouts back.

"Thanks," Emma says bitterly.

"Oh, Emma," he says. "You matter more than my job. You matter more than anything else. You're all I have. But I had to keep my mind occupied—can you understand that? Otherwise I would've gone crazy. You would've lost a father too. I can't get lost in my emotions. It..." His voice wavers again, and Emma can't help but wonder when he clears his throat if it's weakness leaving his body. "It wouldn't be good for anyone if I did that."

"Fine," she says. It doesn't even matter to her. She knows he loves her as much as he possibly can, and if he loves work more, there's not much she can do about it. And what would they have done, sat around in the living room and cried next to each other? Or worse, she cried while he watched her, occasionally checking his phone? "My point is that we have to accept some of the blame."

"How does that help?"

Emma wipes her streaming cheeks. "You're always talking about how important it is to be responsible for our actions. Or our inaction."

"We aren't responsible for Claire driving her car into a goddamn pole."

A vehicle, traveling in the westbound lanes of Interstate 90, veered off the right side of the roadway and struck a utility pole. That's what the accident report said.

"Do you ever picture it?" Emma asks. "Because I can't stop."

"No," Byron says flatly.

"Not the crash," Emma says. "The fire."

There's silence on the other end of the line.

After Claire plowed her car into a pole, the damaged engine exploded. Flames shot up from the hood, then enveloped the interior. An autopsy revealed the cause of death to be asphyxiation. In other words, the crash didn't kill her, and she was breathing when the car caught fire. Claire Isabelle Blake, of New York, New York, burned to death at age twenty-four.

"I see it every time I close my eyes," Byron whispers. "Why do you think I don't sleep anymore?"

"Me too," Emma says.

The grief is unbearable. She digs her fingernails into her palm, wanting to make the hurt physical. But she can't even feel a thing.

"We failed her," Emma says.

She hears a door close, hears her father settle into his office chair. She pictures him looking out the massive window, surveying his domain. Byron gives a long, drawn-out sigh. "No, Emma," he says. "We are not responsible for her death."

"No," Emma agrees. "But we could have been more responsible with her life."

There's silence on the other end, and she hears him get up, start pacing the room. A small smile pulls on the edge of her lip. Knowing where her tic comes from is oddly comforting.

"I looked at my calendar," Byron finally says. "For the day she died, then the week, then the month. I was double, triple booked. I kept looking at it, kept trying to find a spot where I would have had time to reach out, to check in." He stops again, emotion closing this throat.

"And when I realized the opening just wasn't there, I actually felt..." He takes a deep breath. "You'll hate me, Emma, but I actually felt *better.* I didn't feel like I failed her or like I should have done something different. I truly believe that everything I did that day, that week, that month, was important, was something that needed to happen. Claire's problems, they..."

"They what?"

"They were bigger than us, honey," Byron says. "Your mother and I tried. From when she was a little girl, we got her the best therapists, we spared no expense—"

"Yeah, but did you ever talk to her?"

"I'm not a mental health professional."

"No, you were her *father.*"

A few beats of silence pass; the sound of his footsteps stops.

"I'm still her father, Emma. And I'm your father too."

Emma closes her eyes. She can't forgive him, and she can't forgive herself. And when guilt piles on top of grief, the burden is a thousand times heavier. The fear that had been circling around her narrows, tightens into a firm decision.

"You are my father," she agrees. "And you've taught me very well. If working is what helps you grieve, you better get the next few days booked solid."

"Emma, wait—"

She hangs up, then blocks his number.

CHAPTER 41

EMMA'S FEET START taking her around the room again as she loses herself in another conversation with her dead sister. "Did you hear that? I tried, with Dad," she says. "I wonder if you did too."

She pauses at the motel door and peers out the peephole. The afternoon sun glints off the cars in the parking lot. A pair of pigeons squabbles over what looks like the remains of a Big Mac. They're probably going to die from blocked arteries.

"I know you were hurting," Emma goes on. "I know you felt like there was nothing to look forward to. But when did you decide that life was too much? And did you have doubts? Did you drive back and forth on that road, trying to work up the courage to twist the steering wheel? What was it like? How did you finally make that turn?"

A lump rises in her throat. It's as familiar as it is painful. She keeps talking.

"I've read about people who jumped off the Golden Gate Bridge and survived. They say the second they let go of the railing, they knew they'd made a mistake." She shudders when she imagines that long, terrible plunge.

"But you had a chance to undo that first mistake. You crashed your car into the pole, but it didn't kill you. You could've survived. You could've changed your mind. But when the car caught fire, you stayed inside it. 'There was no indication that the victim tried to escape.' That's the worst part of it for me. Knowing that you made the decision to die not once, but *twice*."

And then she's crying too hard to talk anymore.

Claire is the only one who can help her. Except the verb should be past tense.

Claire *was* the only person who could help her. From now on, she's on her own.

CHAPTER 42

The day of the fire

JUST BEFORE DAWN, Emma dreams about her sister. Claire's standing on a hill of snow, wearing a wool hat bright as blood. She's trying to tell Emma something, but the wind snatches away her voice. Emma, barefoot for some reason, tries to run toward her sister, but she keeps breaking through the snow's crust. Stumbling. Falling.

Emma wakes before she reaches Claire, heart pounding like she's actually been running.

Tears sting the corners of Emma's eyes as reality sinks in. Every morning the loss of Claire settles into her chest with a dark, familiar heaviness.

Sometime after nightfall, Emma lay down on the lumpy

bed. For the first time in weeks, she slept through the night. Maybe knowing that she's nearly done—that everything's almost over—allowed her to finally relax.

Emma gets up and brushes her teeth. She's still in her clothes, and though she lost one of her socks in the bed, she doesn't feel like looking for it. She runs her fingers through her tangled hair, slips on her shoes, and hitches her backpack onto her shoulders.

She buys a granola bar from the vending machine and nibbles at it as she walks back toward Ridgemont Academy. It's 6:45. The sun's barely peeking over the horizon. Fog obscures the shapes of buildings, turns birch trees into ghosts. As she nears campus, her steps get slower. Her feet feel like they're made of lead.

Ridgemont was supposed to be a haven: a safe, beautiful place where eager students were taught by accomplished teachers. Where bright young minds were nurtured, strong characters were formed, and the love of learning was fostered.

But it was all such bullshit, wasn't it?

Ridgemont Academy was Type A indoctrination. It didn't teach math or biology so much as it taught students that being the best, no matter what that took, was the only thing that mattered. And if striving to be the best stressed you out, or made you unhappy, then you were weak. You didn't deserve all that you'd been given. She could be as angry at her father as she wanted to be, but the truth is that she is a product of Ridgemont—and she is going to redefine success.

To evade detection by the school's security cameras, Emma avoids the main entrance and doubles back, entering Beecher Forest on the north side of the campus. The woods are full of twisting, narrow paths. Some were made by white-tailed deer, others by students looking for secluded spots to drink contraband beer and make out with their crushes.

Twigs snap softly under her sneakered feet. The forest is spooky, but she clings to the safety of its cover for as long as possible.

She reaches the edge of the Ridgemont meadow just as the pink of dawn is climbing into the sky. On the other side is the cluster of buildings known as Art North; it includes the theater, the concert space, the ceramics studio, and Foster Hall, the media arts building—where the Wi-Fi is strongest.

A wave of relief washes over her. She's so close. It can all end.

She walks across the dewy meadow, moving swiftly but casually—like she's out for a morning stroll. A robin makes a warning call and flutters up from the grass.

She's halfway to the other side when a voice calls out. "Emma? Emma Blake! Stop right there!"

CHAPTER 43

EMMA SPINS AROUND and sprints back toward the woods. She hasn't done anything anyone at Ridgemont has told her to do for months. She sure as hell isn't going to start now.

The gas canister in her JanSport crashes repeatedly against her kidneys as she runs. Wozniak, still shouting, is a hundred yards behind.

"Emma, wait, I just want to talk to you!"

The campus cop is in shape, and Emma gave up on sports a long time ago. She's fifty feet from the woods, then twenty, ten, five. When she slams through the underbrush, the branches of Beecher Forest close behind her, but Wozniak crashes right through them.

"Beecher," she hears Wozniak say into her walkie. "Northeast quadrant."

"Roger," says Jones.

There's no way she can outrun both of them, not with a backpack and the weight of the gasoline canister…which gives Emma an idea. She comes to a screeching halt, leaves sliding out from under her feet. She turns around, drags the JanSport off her back, and yanks the gas can out. Wozniak is just coming around the bend in the path as Emma upends it all over herself.

Wozniak stops dead, hands out, eyes wide.

Jones's staticky voice comes through the walkie. "Woz? You got a visual?"

"Yes," Wozniak says slowly. "She just dumped a gallon of gasoline on herself. And she's holding a lighter."

"Shit, shit, shit," comes Jones's voice. "I'm coming!"

Emma manages a smile as she flicks open the Zippo, but she doesn't draw the flame. She's dripping gasoline, her clothes are stuck to her, the fumes in the air surrounding her are strong. If she strikes the Zippo, she'll go up—and she can't do that with an audience of one.

"Emma!" Wozniak shouts. "Please, listen to me…" She holds her hands out farther, like decreasing the distance between them will make a difference. "Just please, listen."

"Words," Emma gasps, the gas choking her throat. "None of them matter."

CHAPTER 44

"TELL HIM TO stay away," Emma says, motioning toward Wozniak's walkie with the lighter. If he gets here, they'll circle her, and she won't be able to hold them both off. If he gets here, it will increase her audience to two—not nearly enough. If he gets here, she's toast.

Emma giggles at the word choice her brain landed on, a bubble of hilarity rising in her throat, pushing aside the gasoline fumes. Wozniak takes a step toward her.

"Emma," she says. "I know that you think—"

"You don't know shit," Emma screams, the hand with the lighter wobbling. "And if you don't tell him to back off right now, I'll do it, and you'll watch it alone."

Wozniak puts her hands down, reaches for her walkie. "Jones? Where are you? I've got a visual on her, northwest quadrant."

Jones voice comes back, scratchy and confused. "You said northeast? I'm in the northeast."

"Northwest, confirm," Wozniak says, eyes still holding Emma's.

"Northwest, on the way. Just keep her talking."

Wozniak actually rolls her eyes, and Emma feels a pang of sympathy for her, and what it must be like for a female security officer. It'll be even worse for Wozniak once everyone knows that she had Emma cornered and backed off.

"Sorry," Emma says, stepping carefully backward. "I'm not trying to make things harder for you."

"Then don't," Wozniak says, her voice hard and flat. "Just stop."

"Sounds so simple," Emma scoffs.

"That's because it is," Wozniak says, taking another step forward.

"*You* stop," Emma says, raising the lighter. "That's what's simple about this. You stop walking toward me, or I burn."

Wozniak stops, lips thinning, eyes still searching Emma's. "Holy shit," she says. "You're really going to do it, aren't you?"

"Yeah," Emma says, throat clicking as she swallows. "I really am."

Then she turns and runs.

CHAPTER 45

NOSTALGIA HITS EMMA hard as she looks around the newspaper office on the third floor of Foster Hall. Along the east wall are computers with giant monitors for laying out the paper. Three printers, two copy machines, and battered copies of the *AP Stylebook* and the *American Heritage Dictionary* line the south wall. There's a whiteboard for brainstorming story ideas. And a big, dusty monstera plant that the freshmen are in charge of watering, and which consequently is always on the brink of death.

How many late nights has she spent in this room, writing her columns? She could've done it in her room on her laptop, but she loved being in the office, imagining her future as a journalist.

A future that will never happen.

She sits down in her old chair. Considers firing up the desktop and typing a letter to whoever gets on next. *By the time you read this, I'll be gone…*

It's so cliché that she almost laughs.

Whoever found the note would tell the story for the rest of their life. She imagines Prue Bailey, the stoner editor, collaring some poor unsuspecting ninth grader: "You know, a lot people say this room's haunted…"

Emma abruptly stands. Enough reminiscing and fantasizing. It's time to make her video before Jones and Wozniak figure out where she is and batter down the door. She pushes two desks in front of it, just in case. She'd left Wozniak standing in the woods with a horrible decision to make—follow, and be responsible for Emma's suicide, or not follow, and be responsible for Emma's suicide. Emma hopes she'll understand, hopes Wozniak realizes that she's not to blame—the whole world is.

She positions a chair in front of a blank white wall so no one will be able to tell where she is and props her phone on a nearby file cabinet. She shivers slightly, her wet clothes suddenly chilly in the air-conditioned building.

Quickly, she blocks everyone she thinks might try to reach her: Thomas, Jade, Olivia, Celia…Now there will be no interruptions.

Emma steels herself for a second before she opens her

YouTube app and hits the camcorder icon. When she selects GO LIVE, it asks for a title. She types "Emma On Fire."

She clicks PUBLIC. Clicks NEXT. Snaps and uploads a thumbnail photo. Selects GO LIVE again, and the picture on her iPhone goes from black and white to color. She's broadcasting. It's happening.

But for some reason, starting to speak feels harder than holding her arm over the Bunsen burner flame. The seconds tick by. Ten of them, then twenty. Emma swallows. There's a ringing in her ears. How is she supposed to begin? She touches her burn, and the pain brings her back. Reminds her what she's here to say.

"Hi, guys," Emma says. Her voice croaks. She smiles nervously. "Well, here I am. As promised." She glances at the left side of the screen. Already there's a chat.

Omg dont say ur really doin this.

In the upper left corner of her screen, next to the little icon of two heads, is the number six. It means only half a dozen people are watching her.

Emma blinks, and it's twelve. Then twenty-eight. Then seventy-three.

"It's early," Emma says, "but there are a few of you here. Maybe you'll text your friends and tell them to tune in. It'll be like a watch party. The worst one you've ever been a part of." She gives a half smile. "But let's remember that it's going to be a lot worse for me."

438 👥

That was fast.

679 👥

ur so pretty don't unalive urself

Emma can't keep looking at the numbers. She needs to talk. She closes her eyes. Her voice needs to be steady, even if her hands are shaking.

"Irony alert: did you know social media companies know that watching stuff that pisses you off, or freaks you out, or makes you feel bad about yourself keeps you online longer, so that's what they give you? So I guess I'm doing YouTube a favor today. Sorry."

2543 👥

I love you emma on fire

omg emma we were in dance class together when we were three, do you remember me?????????? sara with the sequined tutu

She tucks a strand of wet hair behind her ear. Over six thousand people are watching her now.

"You guys, I'm scared." The sentence flies out of her mouth. She hadn't meant to admit it. But then again, isn't she here to be honest? To tell the truth about everything? "That's because I'm here to burn myself alive. Just like I promised."

u have got 2 b kidding

"And you need to understand that what I'm about to do is not a suicide. It is an act of protest. An act of despair at the state of the world, but of hope too. Because I hope and believe that by doing this, I'll get your attention. I'll encourage you to step up and make things better."

Her hands are shaking even more.

10,377 👥

where is this girl? Someone call 911

Emma I don't know you but I don't want you to do this!!

🙏ing for you

16,002 👥

thought about taking a toaster bath last nite not gunna lie—gotta get as brave as this girl and just do it

18,902 👥

"Catastrophic climate change, which is what we're headed for, will cause species extinction, wars, and global starvation. Endless winter, caused by a nuclear war, would be one way to end global warming, but I'm pretty sure it's not the solution anyone wants."

emma don't do it

this bitch crazy

25,643 👥

28,012 👥

"I know some of you are going to think that this is the ranting of a crazy person. But I'm not crazy. I'm someone who's tired of standing around while humanity destroys itself and everything else on the planet." Emma takes another deep, shuddering breath. "I hope that what I'm about to do will wake you up. Make you take action. I hope that my death means something. *Accomplishes* something."

She feels the sting of tears in her eyes. "I always wanted to be just like my older sister," she says. "But not this time. This time I'm not going to be like Claire. I'm not going to die a lonely, meaningless death. I'm going to go out with a message and an audience."

She reaches for the lighter, holds it in front of the camera.

"I'm going to make a difference."

CHAPTER 46

A BLAST OF Beethoven's Ninth blares from the phone in Peregrine Hastings's hand. He's just been woken by reports that Emma Blake has fled and campus security is pursuing her. He hits the green ACCEPT button. The symphony of his ringtone is replaced by the panicked voice of Thomas Takada.

How did he get this number? Hastings wonders, before what Thomas is saying jolts him even wider awake.

"She's doing it," Thomas yells. "She's streaming!"

Hastings grips his phone, heart pounding. "Where is she?"

"I don't know! I can't tell from the picture."

Hastings races around his bedroom, nearly falls putting on his pants. "Have you tried calling her?"

"It goes right to voicemail."

"Did you leave a message?"

Belt, where is my belt? There, on the dresser. Socks, socks, they don't match, it doesn't matter—

"No one leaves messages, Mr. Hastings! Even if I had, she's not going to listen to it! Not before she—"

"Meet me in the quad. Bring your friends."

"Sir?" Thomas asks.

"She's somewhere on campus, and we need to find her *now.*"

He hangs up. Grabs a shirt from the back of a chair, throws on shoes. He's pulling into the roundabout two minutes later, and in another two he's standing in the dewy grass with a small crowd of terrified-looking students. The birds sing like nothing at all's the matter. It's not even 7:15 a.m.

Thomas steps forward, holding out his phone screen, and Hastings feels his guts twist. He sees Emma Blake, dark eyes blazing, talking right into the camera. He can't make out what she's saying. Next to her, the chat window autoscrolls: fire emojis, crying faces, voices urging her on.

Hastings turns away. "You go to her dorm," he tells Thomas. "Jade, you and Cormac check the library. Celia, the student union. Spencer, James, Pemberly Hall."

He sees Wozniak running up the slope toward them, Jones behind. "I had her," Wozniak gasps. "She was in the woods. I couldn't…I couldn't—"

"Calm down," Hastings says. "Tell me what happened."

But Wozniak can't calm down. Her eyes are wild, her words clipped and frantic. "She's really going to do it, sir. She dumped the gas on herself and told me if I came close she'd light herself. I couldn't…I didn't know what—"

"Where did you see her last?" Hastings asks.

"I followed her as soon as I thought it was safe." Wozniak gulps for air. "But by the time I broke out of the woods in the northeast quadrant, I didn't have a visual on her anymore. I lost her."

"Okay, northeast quadrant," Hastings says. "That's something. That's helpful."

When exposed to heat, the muscles in my thighs will shrink and retract along the shafts of my femur…

He can still remember every line he read in Emma's essay. She's really going to do it.

He pulls his phone from his pocket and dials 911.

CHAPTER 47

EMMA'S GAZE INTO the camera lens is steady. "I'm seventeen years old, and I've already buried my mother and my sister," she says. "The sickness that took my mother's life was breast cancer. The sickness that stole my sister, though, is totally different. It never shows up in an X-ray. It tries to hide itself. But it's spreading."

> *32,987* 👥
>
> holy shit are we in for another pandemic
>
> wtf is she talkin about

Emma wishes everyone would just quit with the chat box. Wishes they'd be quiet and listen. But all she can control is her message.

She takes a long pause. Her throat aches. The words hurt so much to say.

"When my sister, Claire, chose to leave this world, she took all the light with her. There are no words to describe the grief I felt. The grief I still feel."

Emma tries to sit up straighter. Hold her head higher. She knows that pain teaches you things, even if you don't want to learn them.

"Something happens when you're thrust into sudden darkness. You don't go blind. Instead, you start to see things differently," she says. "After Claire died, everything that's messed up about our world was suddenly blazing in front of me, like neon lights against a black background. I saw it all. Hunger. Loneliness. Drought. War."

preach girl

say it louder

#wisdom

🔥🔥🔥🔥

It still hurts to speak. Her body hums with nervous energy. She stares right into the camera. It's the strangest feeling, knowing that so many people are watching her and she can't see any of their faces.

"You know what? We can't fix the world if we're all just looking out for number one. We can't even fix *ourselves.* So I want you to forget about getting into Harvard or pulling in a quarter mil a year by the time you're twenty-five or getting a hundred thousand followers on TikTok. It's not what the endgame should be. The real win is taking care of yourself, and the people you love, and this one beautiful planet we share.

"I didn't do that," she admits. "I played soccer and did well in school and ticked all the boxes, all while my sister was dying inside."

Her mouth is dry. Her palms are sweating.

And someone's pounding on the door.

Emma's heartbeat quickens. "I'm almost done, I swear. Pretty soon you'll get to see what you came to see." She shakes her head like she's disappointed. "But I really want you to listen to what I have to say. Not just watch what I'm going to do. Is that too much to ask? Look at the sacrifice I'm making. For you. Why? To jolt you all into understanding the urgency for change. If my darkness can be a beacon, I'll bear it. For you, for us, for the world. I'll light the darkness with my own fire."

In the middle of her stream, a text window appears. Distracted, she glances at it. Didn't she block everyone she knows?

`Emma, it's Rhaina. I didn't realize. I didn't understand. Everything makes`

sense now. Everything you're saying.
You can be the first. I'll go next.
I'll catch the bus right behind you.
Let's show them. Let's burn.

CHAPTER 48

EMMA GOES QUIET for a moment, forgetting that she's live. The chat's going crazy.

what's happening

lol she realized she forgot the matches

I'm scared

don't do it don't do it don't do it

It's hard for Emma to think right now.

You weren't born weird, okay? Rhaina said. *So take it from someone who was: it's not any fun.*

Emma hadn't paid attention to Rhaina in the hallway, had she? She'd been too busy yelling facts about the climate crisis.

She looks at Rhaina's text again. I'll catch the bus right behind you. Only now does she understand what that means.

"Sorry," she says to her viewers. "Hang on. I just need a second…to think—"

If they both set themselves on fire, the story would go viral beyond Emma's wildest hope. A protest movement that began at Ridgemont would spread throughout the world, faster than any flames.

But Rhaina would be dead, and it would be Emma's fault. Some of the disturbing comments people made on her videos come back to her now. What about that other kid who'd written about catching the bus? And the ones who said they wanted to be as brave as she was? The one comment just today about taking a toaster bath?

What if they, like Claire, felt they couldn't bear to live another day? Then their deaths wouldn't be about protest. They'd be deaths of despair. Deaths that she ushered into existence.

The banging on the door gets louder. She can hear shouting. The doorknob's twisting. The barricade of desks won't keep them out for long.

Emma gathers herself. Turns her attention back to her

live stream. "I'm sorry," she says again. "It turns out that it's kind of complicated to try to kill yourself in front of thirty thousand people—go figure. There are people online telling you to do it. And there are people pounding on your door, screaming at you not to. And then there are others—friends, maybe, or total strangers—who are telling you that they want to do the exact same thing." She swallows. The aching lump stays right where it is. "I don't want anyone to copy me. I want to be the reason the world changes, not the reason a bunch of kids die."

ME ME IMMA DO IT TOO

god is the only perfection repent

CHAPTER 49

EMMA STARES INTO the camera, wishing she could see everyone out there watching. She reaches into the pocket of her backpack. Pulls out the 1933 Zippo that her grandpa bought at a New York auction house and left her in his will. She spins the roller. It sparks, but there's no flame.

"I want to do this," she says quietly. "I've been planning it for months." She holds her wounded arm up to the camera. "I freaking *practiced* for it. But that's because I thought my death might inspire people to fight for their lives. And somehow, instead, it feels like I might inspire more people to die." She leans forward, and her voice is urgent, the hollow feeling in her belly beginning to fill up for the first time since Claire died.

Rhaina is hurting. Rhaina, whom she'd never given a

second thought to, unless it was to make a French horn joke. Rhaina was walking around with all the pain, and all the devastation that Emma herself had—but she was better at hiding it, better at keeping her head down and her mouth shut. Better at pretending everything was just fine... just like Claire.

Emma's breath catches in her throat as she remembers that Rhaina has a little sister. She saw her at freshman orientation, following in Rhaina's path, watching as her older sister pointed out buildings, told her the best places to grab lunch or get a coffee. If Rhaina follows Emma's lead, her little sister will be left holding this feeling, the one that Emma's trying to escape.

And the kid who is going to catch the bus.

And the one with the toaster next to the bathtub.

And their siblings and parents and families and friends will all be left with his horrible, lonely question, *Why?* And even worse, *What could I have done differently?*

Emma's message will catch, she'll go viral in more ways than one. She's not going to inspire people to save the planet or change the course of the human race. She's going to encourage them to die, to spread misery and self-doubt. Emma thinks about Rhaina, how Emma screamed at her about climate change, tearing through the alphabet, rambling about what she thought was important—and completely missing the person right in front of her.

A person who needed help. A person who has a little sister, a family. A person whose loss would hurt the world so much more than she knows. All along, Emma's been missing the big picture; she was trying to save the world, and not helping the people right in front of her. She snaps to attention, eyes refocusing.

"Listen to me, please. This is so important. We can't give up. We may feel hopeless, but we aren't helpless. It's not over yet. Let's decide to take charge. Let's decide to make a change. For my sister. For us. For the whole entire world. One person can make a change, one person *does* make a difference. And that person is you. Watch out for each other. Pay attention. Take care of each other. Ask someone if they're okay."

She lets silence fall for a moment. She snaps the lid down on the lighter, then looks directly at the camera.

"Rhaina, don't do it," she says.

Then she reaches out and taps FINISH with her fingertip.

She bows her head. It's over. She failed.

Slowly she stands up. She pulls the desks away from the door, which immediately swings open, revealing Thomas, Jade, Celia, and Hastings.

Thomas's arms are around her before she even has time to react. Hastings brushes past her to grab her lighter from the floor, where she dropped it. "We need to get you to a hospital," he says.

"You don't," she says. "I'm fine. I'm really, truly okay. I'm not a danger to myself, or to anyone else. I mean that. I was...I was wrong. I shouldn't have made those threats. I didn't realize what they would do to other people."

Hastings, whose hair is sticking up all over and whose shirt looks like it has been wadded up in a corner, stares hard at Emma's face, searching for signs of deception. She stares right back. She can see worry, still etched into his brow. And a glimmer of hope in his watery blue eyes.

"You need to find Rhaina," she says urgently. "Rhaina Johnson, I think she lives in Briar. She's not okay."

Hastings nods, pulls out his phone.

"And Olivia, my roommate," Emma says, words flowing more easily now. "She's not okay either. She's got an OnlyFans, she's trying to help pay for tuition. Maybe you could find a scholarship so she doesn't feel like she has to—"

"Dear Lord," Hastings says, his hand coming up to his forehead. "Okay, thank you, Emma. Thank you for looking out for others. Wozniak and Jones are on the way to Rhaina's room right now. Olivia we can deal with later, but right now, you are my biggest concern, and my most important responsibility—and we need to get you to a hospital."

She steps away from Thomas's embrace. "I understand," she says, nodding. She knows all about responsibilities, about what it's like to have everyone looking at you to make things right.

She turns to Jade, whose face is pale and tear-streaked.

"I thought you were really going to do it," Jade says. "God, Emma, I was so scared."

"Me too," Emma says quietly. Then she turns to the small crowd. "Thank you. Really…I just…" But her words are gone now, and she's just left looking at their faces, and being thankful for each and every one of them.

"You don't have to talk," Celia says, reaching out for her hand. Her nose wrinkles. "But you do totally need a shower."

CHAPTER 50

THE WORLD IS so green and bright. Its beauty hurts her eyes. Emma feels like she's floating down the path. Every cell in her body feels like it's charged with electricity, with new and ferocious life. They kept her overnight at the hospital. Her father was by her side the whole time, eerily silent without his phone, which he'd left in his car. Instead, he held her hand, only letting it go when he brought her back to campus this morning.

She's only dimly aware of where she's walking. She has no plan for what happens next. She feels like she's woken up from a dream.

Yesterday was supposed to be the end. Instead it was a beginning. Of what she isn't sure yet. A life without Claire. But a life that will mean something. A life where Rhaina is okay, and she knows that the little ripples she causes by doing good things for one person will spread, eventually affecting the entire world.

She sees Ridgemont students walking to breakfast, laughing with each other like nothing has ever been wrong. For the first time in months, Emma doesn't want to tell them that they're doomed.

Because what if, somehow, they aren't? What if, every time someone told her things were going to be okay, and she just sneered—what if *she* was the one who was wrong?

A robin hops along the path beside her for a moment, then flutters up into a tree. She stops and looks up, wanting to find her nest. She's peering dazedly into the branches when Rachel Daley appears by her side, talking a mile a minute, questions shooting out of her mouth like bullets, her phone held out to capture an audio clip.

Emma flinches away. But she catches a strange look in the reporter's eye. And Emma suddenly realizes that Rachel Daley is disappointed.

Emma speaks softly, her voice full of wonder. "You secretly wanted me to die, didn't you?"

Rachel stops the recording app, shakes her head. "No, Emma, listen—"

"Not to you," Emma says, spinning away. "You just want a headline. You don't actually care about me. The real story is that I didn't die, that I chose life and kindness, and caring for others. I know it's not the front page. I know it's not above the fold. But *that's* the story. Print *that*."

And Emma walks away beneath the magnolia trees. Free.

Hopeful.

Alive.

CHAPTER 51

Dear Claire,

I told my therapist that we used to write letters. She said I should keep doing it, because supposedly it'll help me process my feelings. She said I needed to write everything down.

My assignment today is to recall a happy memory. (In case you wondered, it's the only kind of assignment I'm doing. My teachers said I could take incompletes this semester and finish up during the summer. Believe it or not, it was Hastings's idea.) So anyway, here's a memory from a long time ago.

It was my fifth birthday, and Mom and Dad had rented a big white tent for the backyard. It was like they were hosting a wedding! There were bouquets of balloons, towers of cupcakes, and multicolored streamers hanging from the trees. There was a clown on a unicycle and a little pony we could ride, and every kid in the neighborhood was there, and they were all screaming their heads off in delight.

At first I felt like a princess. Everything was so big and bright and wonderful, and it was all for me. But it didn't take very long before I started to feel really small and really lost. Everything was such an expensive spectacle. I was five—did my party really need waiters? Hand-calligraphed place cards? A Pocket Lady, handing out presents from her giant skirt? There were so many people at my party, and half of them I'd never even seen before. I'd lost our parents in the crowd.

And then you came out of nowhere and found me, hiding behind a rosebush, and you picked me up and you carried me to the far corner of the garden. "Here," you said, "I made this for you, Emmie. Happy birthday." And you set me down next to a tiny, beautiful house constructed out of sticks and leaves, glass beads and glitter glue. "This is a fairy house, and soon there will be fairies living in it," you said to me. "You might not ever see them, but they'll be watching over you, granting you little wishes, and keeping you safe."

It was the best present I ever got.

It's too late for these wishes, but I'm making them anyway:

I wish I could've made you a fairy house, Claire.

I wish I could've kept you safe.

And I wish you could call me and tell me how to go on. Instead I've got to fumble through life without you.

I will never understand why you did what you did, and it will never be okay.

But I'm going to have to try to be okay.

I realize that if I'm going to write everything down, like I'm supposed to, it'd never fit in a letter. It'd have to be more like a whole book. A book about a girl who wanted to save the world but only ended up saving herself.

It doesn't sound like much of an accomplishment, does it? But maybe that's all anyone's really able to do anyway. Oh, Claire, I wish you could've saved yourself. I wish you had chosen to live.

The world is smaller without you in it. It's also worse.

But I'm going to try to make it better, for others, and for myself.

I miss you. I love you.

Forever and always,
your little sister

AUTHOR'S NOTE

When I was eighteen years old, I started working at McLean Hospital, the psychiatric affiliate of Harvard Medical School. The job was as a psych aide, assisting in medical care under the watchful eye of doctors, nurses, and psych techs. I applied because I needed employment after high school, and I think they hired me because they saw I had empathy for people, and a desire to spend time chatting with patients and listening to their stories. I made friends there whom I still think about to this day.

If you or someone you know is experiencing thoughts of suicide, self-harm, or other mental health issues, you don't have to struggle alone. Trusted medical professionals and many organizations can provide help and resources. Here are a few organizations and websites you can visit to learn more:

- American Academy of Child & Adolescent Psychiatry (aacap.org)

- Crisis Text Line (crisistextline.org)
- Go Ask Alice! (goaskalice.columbia.edu)
- National Alliance on Mental Illness (nami.org)
- National Institute of Mental Health (nimh.nih.gov)
- National Suicide Prevention Lifeline (suicidepreventionlifeline.org)
- Nemours Teens Health (kidshealth.org/en/teens/your-mind)
- Suicide & Crisis Lifeline (988lifeline.org/chat)
- Teen Line (teenline.org)
- Warmline (warmline.org)

James Patterson

ABOUT THE AUTHORS

James Patterson is the most popular storyteller of our time. He is the creator of unforgettable characters and series, including Alex Cross, the Women's Murder Club, Jane Smith, and Maximum Ride, and of breathtaking true stories about the Kennedys, John Lennon, and Tiger Woods, as well as our military heroes, police officers, and ER nurses. Patterson has coauthored #1 bestselling novels with Bill Clinton, Dolly Parton, and Michael Crichton. He has told the story of his own life in *James Patterson by James Patterson* and received an Edgar Award, ten Emmy Awards, the Literarian Award from the National Book Foundation, and the National Humanities Medal.

Emily Raymond worked with James Patterson on *First Love* and *The Lost,* and is the ghostwriter of six young adult novels, one of which was a #1 *New York Times* bestseller. She lives with her family in Portland, Oregon.

For a complete list of books by

JAMES PATTERSON

VISIT

JamesPatterson.com

Follow James Patterson on Facebook
JamesPatterson

Follow James Patterson on X
@JP_Books

Follow James Patterson on Instagram
@jamespattersonbooks

Follow James Patterson on Substack
jamespatterson.substack.com

Scan here to visit JamesPatterson.com and learn about giveaways, sneak peeks, new releases, and more.